T0354676

Remember

Remember

THE SONG THAT KEEPS THE SOUL ALIVE

SRIPARNA SAHA

PARTRIDGE

ISBN: Hardcover   978-1-4828-8709-9
           Softcover   978-1-4828-8707-5
           eBook   978-1-4828-8708-2

Print information available on the last page.

To order additional copies of this book, contact
Partridge India
000 800 10062 62
orders.india@partridgepublishing.com

www.partridgepublishing.com/india

CONTENTS

CONTENTS

For Di

As she encouraged me to write this story;

For my Ma and Baba

For having faith in me and always supporting me;

And if you are reading this, you would know this is

for you, 'Ansh'

Why exactly did I fall for you…?
I wonder why
So deeply, so insanely
Was it because how our long conversations
Satiated my searching soul
In this wilderness of chaos?
Or how peacefully our silence hummed its own
    tune?
Why exactly did I love us?
Perhaps it was the gentle touch—
Yours on my soul
Holding me
Ever so slightly—breathing life in me.
Perhaps it was the silent smile on your lips that
    did the trick—
Melting away under my gaze.
Why exactly did the departure hurt so?
So much that it tugged at my soul
With tears in our eyes and smiles on our lips
Is something that perhaps I might never know?
Why exactly…?
We were like shooting stars,
Brought together for a moment—to be separated
    for an eternity
Why do I cry and smile together—thinking of you
Is something I will never know?

CHAPTER 1

Letting Go

A s she sat looking at the night sky full of twinkling stars, sipping tea from the earthen mug and took in the smell emanating from the mixture of the tea and the mug, she seemed to travel back in time—thinking of the beautiful rainy days when she would just sit by the window, watching as the raindrops cast beautiful asymmetrical patterns on the glass window, and the wild cuckoo would call distantly as if trying to break into her train of thoughts; of the dark nights when the glimmer of the distant sky was the only source of light in the darkened surroundings of the city life, when load-shedding was a common occurrence in the lazy summer evenings. She had come a long way, far from those memories that shaped her life. Yet always, a feeling of un-contentment had unsettled and chased her.

Her life had been split between her dreams, her ambitions, and her soul that just wanted peace in the minutiae of life. She always felt that she had been chasing the unknown and that her search for peace would never culminate into happiness, until she came to Dehradun—a town where the evening brought with it silence, away from the cacophony of the city life. At times she wondered if she was affected by the need to turn back into the medieval times, resonating within her soul to slow down. This town, where she could spend her time looking up at the twinkling stars, wondering if she had committed a mistake giving up her city life, her prestigious job and all the worldly pleasures just for the contentment of her soul. But now that she was here, she could chose to be anyone she wanted.

It was here that she met Ansh.

The thought brought a smile to her lips. Sweet and adorable Ansh, so full of life with his mischievous eyes filled with laughter. He could make anyone smile with his stupid jokes. It was difficult not to fall in love with him. And she couldn't resist the same. Nor had she tried to. Her relationship with him was different yet beautiful. They became good friends, and then moved on to be lovers. It had been the happiest phase of her life. Lately, she had started to notice the slight changes his behavior, like the gentle fraying of a cloth, holding on strong but it was hard to tell when it would give away completely. The bipolar disorder was at times bringing out shades in him that made Maya wonder if he was the same person she had fallen in love with. Today was the first night away from him since she had met him six months back and it was difficult for her to imagine a life without him. She felt that her life would turn when she had agreed to let him go. The silence of the night stretched longer as the weight of her decision was gradually sinking in.

She was jerked back into reality as the siren of the ambulance shattered the silence of the night air. She traced her steps back into the eerily silent hospital ward where Ansh lay. After the accident two months back, he had been in a vegetative state. Day and night she had prayed with fervor that Ansh would recover and be back to his usual self. It was the sheer determination of her faith that kept the doctors trying. But time had run out when the doctors explained to her that Ansh's systems were failing and that they could just keep him alive artificially. Maya had been in a dilemma, thinking if she could bear the burden of deciding to release him from his life, however unbearable it might be. She had turned their apartment upside down, torn through each shelf of Ansh's study trying to find some address, some source through which she could contact his family. The sheer desperation of the situation had driven her crazy. She had caught hold of a number from one of his journals, but then each time she had called at that number, it was answered by an automated voicemail that said something about St. Paul's orphanage. Ansh had never spoken much about his family, and she cursed herself for not coercing him to talk about his family more.

She remembered the first time that she had met him and realized that he would never have wanted to live on like this—unable to cherish the small joys under the sun. And then she realized it was time to let go of him. It had been an hour since they had pulled him off the artificial respirator. An hour since she had lost the person who had come to mean everything to her. But looking at his peaceful face, she didn't feel a twinge of regret for being in love with him; nor did she want to change the way their love had been.

Miles away from the city life, away from the probing eyes of friends and family, this stranger had taught her what she had been searching for throughout her life—no matter what, she will always remember where it all started from.

This hiatus
Could be a short-lived one, I hope.
But even if our paths never cross again
I will carry your memories in my heart—
A piece of you embedded in my soul.
All our wordless conversations and quiet smiles
The feel of your hand gently holding onto mine—
will be imbibed in my being.
For they say goodbyes are hard,
But if it is inevitable
I hope you carry a piece of me in your soul...
A piece of me within you.

CHAPTER 2

Life After You

It had been a week since Ansh had left, a week since Maya had been trying to gather the fragments of the life he left behind and start afresh. But all of it seemed so impossible to her, this simple act of moving on. How is one expected to move on, after being left behind, not in life, but after death? His smiles haunted her day and night. Sometimes hours passed before she woke up to a dark dreary room and it seemed that the room reflected the darkness that she felt in her soul. Each corner of her house had small pieces of them together—it was there in the half-torn red paper kite that they flew together that subtly hung on the lampshade; or the hand impressions that they had so lovingly painted on her bedroom wall. She still remembered how surprised she had been when Ansh had first suggested to her to move-in with him. But after giving it a thought she hadn't found it weird. In-fact that had seemed the most plausible thing to do. Those memories….were so beautiful she thought as she glanced at the bedside picture frame that held the memories of the day when they had finally moved in together. Both of them had been lying exhausted on the bed when Ansh had clicked that picture.

Maya knew that Ansh would have hated seeing her like this, and each night before she went to bed she asked him to forgive her for not being able to live on like he would have wanted. Time seemed to have attained an intangible aspect for her, where it did not matter whether it was early morning or dusk. She had been delaying reading through his journals and diaries ever since she had found them in their study. Once she had playfully started reading though his diary, and Ansh had gone mad with anger.

At times Maya felt that Ansh's personality was shrouded in a veil, a deep dark abyss that seemed to evade her each time she tried to reach out to him. Those were the times that she was scared. But then he would be his normal self, smiling, playful, and he seemed like a child with no worries under the sun. She looked at the pile of letters that had poured into her mailbox, the ones she hadn't bothered going through. But tonight, by sheer will she decided to go through each one of them. Most of them looked ordinary, but a big cream-colored envelope caught her eye. Nothing seemed special about it, except for the fact that it wasn't addressed to her. She battled in her own mind, thinking if she should open his letter. When Ansh was alive, they had often fought about how each one of them wanted to be the first to open their own mails and had in fact come up with the pact that they would leave the other's mail untouched. She wondered if death had changed that pact.

After thinking for a long time, she finally decided to open the envelope. It contained a letter addressed to Ansh from his sister. In their short time together, Ansh had never mentioned a lot about his family, except for the fact that he loved them dearly, but due to differences in ideologies had chosen a life away from them. Maya felt sick to the stomach, thinking that his family wasn't even aware that their beloved Ansh was no longer a part of this earth. Maya felt lost at the bad timing—if the letter could have arrived a week earlier, she could have written back to them telling them about Ansh's condition, asking them to come over. But Ansh had always been so secretive about his past. She had even joked at times that perhaps he was suffering from a personality disorder where he was trying to hide his past. Ansh had gone silent and had later told her that he had been diagnosed with a bipolar personality disorder in his childhood.

Maya had been careful ever since not to push him too hard. She wanted to be there for him, she wanted him to be able to overcome this difficult situation, and she wanted to be able to help him. If only she had known that he had been thinking of something this severe, she could have made him change his mind. She could have convinced him not to jump off the cliff that afternoon. When she had received the call from the hospital late in the evening, it had been too late. The damage had been irreversible, they told her, his injuries too severe to be cured.

She thought of promptly writing back at the address, at Hardwar, which seemed to scream at her from the top of the envelope. She was still groping with her own grief and didn't feel that she was ready to encounter his family, which was practically unknown to her. The letter pleaded Ansh to come back once—his little sister was getting married in less than a year. Maya's eyes filled with tears at the irony of the entire situation, at the hope that emanated from the letter and the dismal gloom that surrounded her.

Ansh had been living away from his family for more than three years now. She had come to know this from one of their friends who worked at the small town library where

Maya was a frequent visitor. She tried to decide that going that extra mile to visit his family and let them know about him would be too much of a trial for her. But as she caught a glance of his smiling face looking at her from the picture frame beside her bed, she knew she had to do this for him. For Ansh was always the one who lived life on its edges, full of laughter, full of life itself. It was funny how life had struck back at him, reduced him to its mercy for the past two months.

Maya had decided that she would visit his family the next day, and tell them about their and her loss. She still groped with her own inability to forgive Ansh for what he had done to himself and her. Her mind was still clouded with thoughts of what she would say to his little sister, so full of hope of his return when she finally fell asleep.

*Someday when you will be no more than a
     memory—*
Locked away in the depths of my heart;
*Someday when hearing your name wouldn't mean
     skipping heartbeats.*
Some day—
When I in all my nascent stages wouldn't think
How beautiful things had been with you.
I'll know that I have moved on.
But that moment is not this
And with all my fervor –
*I can still hear my heart respond to the rhythm of
     your*
Name.

CHAPTER 3

The Visit

The one-and-a-half-hour drive to Hardwar where Ansh's family lived seemed monotonous to Maya. As scenic as it might have been, but for her, everything seemed to have acquired just different shades of gray. Just three months back, the lush green banyan trees on either side of the roads would have given Maya a sense of peace and serenity, but Ansh's death seemed to have taken away with it all the colors which bordered at the brink of her consciousness. She still wasn't sure of how she would break the news to his family. She had spent the last forty-five minutes sitting in her car, parked outside the address on the envelope. Several people had walked passed her car, without even giving it a second glance. She got off her car, and stood outside the huge wooden gate that isolated the house from her view. Maya gathered up the vestiges of courage left inside her and decided to ring the bell.

A middle aged man, probably the gardener (she assumed from the pair of scissors held in his hand), opened the door. For Maya, it seemed like an eternity had come to a stop.

Here she was, going to step into a world, a life Ansh had left behind—a life that she could never be a part of. It took her a while to realize that the man was asking her something, probably wanting to know the reason for her arrival there in this sultry summer afternoon to interrupt him in his work. She choked on her words, before she could ask, 'Is this Ansh's house?'

A look of bewilderment came over the man's face, something that she couldn't comprehend. Not getting any answer, she was about to leave when a sweet and melodious voice reached out to her, 'Kaka, who's there?'

She turned back to find a young girl of around twenty-one standing near the doorway. Her beautiful eyes seemed to be filled with joy, a joy that spelled excitement and eagerness. She must be Tara, Ansh's sister. She had gathered that from her letter to Ansh.

She asked, 'Are you Tara?'

'Yes. But I did not recognize you?' replied Tara.

How was she supposed to know Maya?

'Hi! Tara! I am Maya—'

She had barely spoken out when Tara rushed to her and swept Maya into an embrace.

'So finally we meet. Where is Ansh? Did he send you alone? Oh my God, I just can't believe it—I finally get to meet you. Ansh told us that he has a new friend Maya and he would write about you in almost all his letters. I was very eager to meet you and so is my mom. After all, the only friend we've seen in his life is Vivaan. So meeting you is a welcome change.'

'Ansh is not here with me', Maya replied.

If Tara was bewildered at her response, she gave no inkling of it. She was too lost in her own excitement to notice the silence that surrounded Maya, to notice the lifelessness that oozed out from her. Tara dragged her inside the house telling the gardener to close the door behind them. Ansh had probably mentioned something about them to Tara in his letters, she gathered from the way Tara received her. As she took in the welcoming interiors, her eyes stopped at the familiar face smiling down at her from the life-size picture frame. As she inched closer, she could feel the tears that threatened to fail her.

'Ansh', she whispered.

'Vivaan', Tara chimed in.

Maya looked on, not understanding clearly. 'He is Vivaan' pointing to the smiling face that Maya knew to be Ansh.

'And that is Ansh,' pointing to an unfamiliar face.

For a moment, Maya was lost and her head started reeling at the confusion. The last thing she remembered before she dropped unconscious was ~~Ansh's,~~ and not Vivaan's face that looked on from the picture.

When light fades,
And the dusk creeps in
I hear the faint sound of wings
Beating to the rhythm of life.
And if the darkness threatens to stain the wings of
   life
I'll follow just…
The whisper of my heart.

CHAPTER 4

Unfamiliar Faces

When Maya opened her eyes, she found herself in an unfamiliar room. The first thing she noticed was how the entire room had a touch of creation—of sheer creativity. Sunlight streamed in through the glass window and cast huge patterns on the floor. The ceiling looked as if it had been painted to resemble the night sky—different hues of blue adorned the ceiling. A canvas stand stood in one corner. She noticed different paintings adorned the wall—some in charcoal and some in watercolor.

She could not remember what had caused her to pass out and then she realized how Tara had referred to the unknown face in the picture as Ansh. Maya felt really lost, as if she had entered a maze without a bargain, without an idea of how to break through. She knew very little about 'Ansh's' family she agreed, but now she wondered who Ansh really was. Tara walked in with an older woman, whom Maya assumed to be her mother.

'Maya! Are you all right? You just passed out', enquired Tara.

'I feel better. I think it's the heat', she replied.

'Maya, this is my mother', Tara explained, looking at her confused expression. 'For the past six months, Ansh has been in regular touch with us over letters. I never understood why would someone do that, especially now with Facebook and WhatsApp being so accessible. I never knew he was so much like Vivaan… Ansh wrote to us frequently and he told us all about you. I am wondering why he sent you alone. After all, it's his sister's wedding. He should be here', continued Tara.

Maya was certain that there had been some confusion. She decided to stay quiet and find out more about Ansh—who he was? The person whom she had met six months back in Dehradun, or the person whom Tara referred to as Ansh in the picture below.

Ansh's mom, she noticed, had a kind face, full of affection as she came forth and embraced Maya.

'You don't know it is such a relief to see you here. I somehow feel that you brought Ansh back into our lives… we had been trying so hard to get him to come back and meet us… Even after his father passed away, he did not come back… I had lost all hope of seeing my son again…' her voice choked.

Maya had no response to that. She was utterly bewildered at what was going on around her. She didn't even know Tara or her mom, or even their son Ansh (???). All she knew was that face… ~~Ansh's~~ face. No, Vivaan's face. Maya wanted to hide herself in a cocoon and shut off from everyone around her. Mistaking her silence as discomfort, Ansh's mom left the room saying she had to go and take care of some preparations for the wedding and asked her to rest.

As soon as her mother left the room, Maya said, 'Tara, I need to talk to you. It is kind of important.'

'Yes?'

'Who was the other person—Vivaan—in the picture below?'

'He is Ansh's childhood friend. Why, didn't Ansh tell anything about his past to you before? I agree that we had our differences in the past. After dad passed away, we tried hard to ask him to come back. But he never bothered to reply. But six months back, his letter arrived and since then we've been in touch. Don't worry, now that you are here, we'll make up for all the lost time.'

'Where does Vivaan stay?' Maya cut in.

'In Dehradun', said Tara.

The entire situation just seemed to be bizarre. The timing of the letters seemed to match with when she had met Ansh. But then why did he hide his identity from her? Posing as Ansh... And where was the real Ansh? Maya had come to this city with her life full of questions, but it seemed that the questions were never ending. She now felt that if she told Tara about Ansh/Vivaan's death, they would perceive her to be crazy. She asked Tara if she could get Vivaan's address or contact number.

Tara told her that she could ask Ansh directly when he came home. Maya felt that if anyone could answer her questions and help her make sense of the entire situation it would be the real Ansh himself. But then she wondered what would she say to him? What would she ask him? She was extremely engrossed in her thoughts when the honks of a car brought her attention back to the present. She found herself staring absent-mindedly into a plate full of biscuits served with tea.

And Tara's delighted scream came floating through the room, calling out to her. Maya walked outside the room to find a tall, disheveled-looking man, hugging Tara. She took in his white shirt, and the blue denims he wore, and deduced that he must have travelled a lot and looked exhausted. Before she could turn away, Tara pointed to her, and their eyes met.

Where Maya's eyes were full of questions, she could read the sadness in his eyes. Tara's voice cut in through the silence and restlessness that seemed to have enveloped them.

'Maya, look who's here,' said Tara.

Before she could compose herself, Maya found herself face to face with the stranger from the photograph. The same stranger who was supposed to be Ansh.

Ansh, whose memories she had decided to bury into the small town of Dehradun.

Ansh, whom she had decided to let go?

The tales that float in your eyes
Do not reflect loss and pain.
Instead I see a million dreams lighten up
The hazel of your eyes each time I look inside.
You exude warmth and serenity-
If only I knew what goes on inside those flickering
*   eyelids-*
Each time you hide your pain with a
Smile.

CHAPTER 5

Ghosts

After Tara left the room, silence settled as a veil around Maya and Ansh. The recognition in his eyes, told Maya that he had answers to the questions that brimmed in her eyes.

'Ansh?' Maya finally spoke the name she had so lovingly remembered till this morning, but now it felt like a predicament of doom.

'I am sorry…' started Ansh.

Maya felt a sudden surge of anger build up inside her. She was mourning the loss of her ~~Ansh,~~ no Vivaan, and this stranger who supposedly was the real Ansh and had the audacity to offer her his apologies. All the pain, anger that was pent up inside her, burst forth and she slapped Ansh really hard.

'Sorry? Are you mourning the loss of your beloved friend, who lied and cheated me? Or are you sorry that your lies did not die along with him?' retorted Maya.

The look of pain and helplessness that crossed his eyes confused Maya even more.

'You have all the right to be angry. But would it be too much if I ask you to hear me out? Vivaan loved you—' Ansh said, but Maya cut him short.

'And yet he chose to lie to me? Lie about his identity? I loved that man with all my soul, and today when he is gone, I don't even have the memories to look back to, because everything around him was a lie. He was always so secretive about his past, and when I found some link to his past, I get to know that everything was a lie. If I hadn't decided to come here, I would have lived my entire life believing him', said Maya as her voice became hoarse and she choked on the tears that rose in her.

'I can explain everything to you. And then I will let you decide if you choose to forgive Vivaan and me. But whatever Vivaan did was on my insistence. Can we go somewhere else and talk?' said Ansh.

Maya nodded, not trusting her voice anymore.

'I know this is hard on you, and you want this to be over soon. Trust me, I would give anything in this world to bring Vivaan back, if I had a chance. But with Tara's wedding preparations on, I don't think I can sneak out of the house before evening, given that I haven't been here in three years. We can go to the bank of Ganges in the evening for a walk and talk there', he put in.

'I don't want to stay here. Just looking at your face will remind me of the lies hidden underneath, lies that you and your beloved friend Vivaan chose to tell everyone around you. I have my car parked outside. I will meet you at the Ghat around five o'clock this evening', replied Maya.

Ansh did not try to convince her to stay, but walked her to the car.

As she started the engine, Ansh knocked at the window and said, 'He loved you dearly, Maya. I know he was not a much sorted person, but don't let this situation scar his love for you.'

His words echoed in her ears as faint as the chimes of the temple bells that rang in the background of life here in Hardwar, as she drove past the house that seemed to be another broken link to her past—a past which bordered on the brink of becoming a lie.

Underneath the tough exterior of
Sophistication
Lies a complex web of judgments,
You dismiss the efforts of others as farce;
You easily accept that people often wear masks.
The simple fact evades you—
This tangled web of imperfections makes us alive.
And brings people together as their own.
These imperfections

CHAPTER 6

The Jigsaw of Life

A s Ansh watched her drive away, he felt a wave of helplessness crush him. Three years... He had been away... from everyone he loved... his family, his best friend... the life he was fond of... The life he had chosen... And today when he was back, a major part of his life had transformed in ways that he couldn't put it back together again...

Would Maya even understand the twist of fate that he and Vivaan had been through? She would perhaps hate him forever, for swapping his identity with Vivaan. But at that time, it was the only thing that seemed feasible. Vivaan and Ansh always had each other's back—their friends used to say. But today he felt lost, alone and incomplete.

Vivaan was more than a friend to him. He was like his own brother. They had seen each other through their best and through their worst phases. When Vivaan was struggling through his own depression, Ansh had been there to support him, bring him back to being the person who always cherished life. And when Ansh had decided to follow his own dreams, it was Vivaan who had stood by him.

Such was their bond... their friendship. He had gone to Dehradun hoping to find everything as it had been when he had left. He had wanted to explain to Vivaan, why all his letters, emails and texts had gone unattended. True that the house they had rented together was still the same. But when he walked into it, early that morning, a lot more than just the interiors had changed. Maya and Vivaan had seemed so happy in the picture that looked out at him from the living room wall, but the apartment itself had a dismal gloom in the air. And then he spotted Vivaan's picture with a garland around it.

When he had walked into his house today, little did he know that he would meet Maya in person. He had read about her in all the letters that he had found at his own place before he left for Dehradun yesterday. Her simplicity and the pain in her eyes had stirred something inside his own soul.

As he traced his steps back into his house, Ansh felt he had a lot to catch up to. After losing Vivaan, Ansh realized the true worth of relations in life. He had not been able to come to the last rites of even his own father. Even though it would take time, Ansh decided he wouldn't abandon his family ever again. He wanted to be there.

If only he hadn't left for Rajasthan that night... He felt perhaps that their lives would still be sorted. He still needed to know how Vivaan died... Was it the depression yet again? Only one person in this world had the answers to all his questions...

Maya.

What is it about you that draws attention?
Your skin tone—the color of peach and honey
blended together?
Or the depth of emotions that shrouds you in a
veil…
What is it about you that is so tangible?
Yet you evade the grasp of people who wish to
hold on to you—trying to bind you to the
essence of life.
Perhaps you –
Are like the light—that oozes out of the thin,
cracked, crumbling walls,
Light that cannot be restrained,
You radiate gold
And in that lies the essence of your existence.
You are the
TRUTH

CHAPTER 7

Pieces of Truth

As Maya sat on the banks of the river Ganga, the chiming of the temple bells and the chants of the various hymns floating through the air, her mind wandered off, trying to grope bits of memories which danced like the vibrant colors of a kaleidoscope in the panorama of her vision. Had she been so naïve that she had overlooked some small hint that might have given away Vivaan's lie? Why did her life have to be so complicated always? She had been missing her mother even more since she had come across Ansh's and Vivaan's lies. How she wished she could talk to her once. She had never thought that her father would remarry after her mother's death six years back. But in the course of time, she had grown distant with her father. Her mother had been the only true source of strength that she ever had. With ~~Ansh~~ Vivaan gone, she had again lost the person whom she had started to trust and love. She couldn't believe that she had let Ansh—the real one, to convince her to listen to what he had to say. Perhaps she still wanted to believe that there had been some reason that had led Vivaan to lie to her. It is indeed strange how the mind plays tricks, trying to drown the voice of reason, which clearly told her to go back to Dehradun that very moment.

She glanced at her wristwatch; the golden colored hands blaringly signaled that Ansh would be arriving soon. She had started feeling a restlessness nestle up inside her soul, her mind unable to focus on anything. She wanted this ordeal to be over soon. She was lost deep in her thoughts when Ansh walked up to her. He wore a white shirt, loosely tucked into the light denim trousers. He had a disheveled look on his face, his eyes frantic, as if he was searching for something. For a moment, Maya felt her heart melting. True that she was deeply in love with 'Vivaan' and had lost him, but this man who stood in front of her, loved Vivaan as his own brother, and perhaps his loss was equivalent. Ansh stood looking at her like a convict whose destiny rested on her next words.

'Hi, Ansh', Maya flinched as she spoke. The memories related with this four-letter word were immense and she could feel her heart squeeze into a tiny ball at the pain that followed.

'Maya', Ansh said, settling down beside her.

'I know all this has been very difficult for you to understand. It is a rather difficult situation. But believe me it has been difficult for me as well,' he continued.

'Then why this entire pretense? What could be so significant that someone chooses to hide his own identity?' Maya interjected.

'Let me explain. Vivaan was my childhood friend. We literally grew up together. Did he ever tell you about his family?' Ansh asked.

'No, I just knew that there had been some major issues with his dad, after which he moved out and went to Dehradun', Maya replied.

'That's partly true. Vivaan never told you about his family because he didn't have one. Vivaan was an orphan; he grew up at an orphanage that was the only home that he knew. He was a talented writer, and he won a scholarship to study in the school I went to. We were in sixth grade then, when I met him first. He was so hardworking and talented that he won scholarship to study there each year thereon. We became a part of each other's lives, more than friends— we were like brothers. After our class 12th exams we both got into the same college. Vivaan always wanted to be a writer; he knew what he wanted to do with his life. But then something happened that changed everything. That changed Vivaan...' He trailed.

'Vivaan was quite popular in our batch because he was very good with words. People could relate to his writing, and made him a favorite. He participated in mostly all the inter-college competitions that were organized, and he won most of them. He was working on a story for one of the competitions. Another guy, Rajat, who was our senior, was participating in the same competition. He was the son of my father's friend. He wanted Vivaan to withdraw his name from the competition. When he didn't, they stole Vivaan's story and gave it away to a local newspaper to be published under Rajat's name. When Vivaan submitted the same for the competition, not only was his writing rejected, but he was also blamed for plagiarism. We didn't have any proof to prove otherwise. What followed was a period of depression in his life, where he seemed to have lost all purpose. Nothing could motivate him anymore. He always wanted to be a writer, but he stopped writing altogether after that', continued Ansh.

'It was at that time that the trouble started. He would get violent at times, ready to almost kill, and then after some time he would be perfectly normal…'

'I really don't understand whatever you are trying to say', said Maya.

'Please, listen. Vivaan recovered gradually, but still there was something amiss. He had been diagnosed with bipolar disorder in his childhood. Two years passed and we graduated. I wanted to be a painter. I wanted to soar up high in the sky, away from all bounds. When my dad came to know this, he made every possible effort to make me change my mind. He wanted me to take over his business. I had been trying to put together an exhibition of my paintings, and wanted some renowned artists to come and have a look at my work and see if I had some potential.

When my dad came to know this, he stooped really low and sabotaged my exhibition. He hired some people to burn my paintings the night before the exhibit. He felt he could force me to become a slave of his desires. But I had decided to take time off travelling and painting in the wilderness. I wanted to be inspired by nature, and used that as the theme for my next set of paintings. In the meantime, Vivaan was looking for a retreat and was seriously thinking about taking up writing as a profession. So we both moved to Dehradun, and we decided to swap our identities. That way he could write under my name, Ansh, and I could paint as Vivaan. This worked for both of us fine, as we both needed anonymity to get our work established, and we decided we would hold on this façade till both of us had achieved our dreams', completed Ansh.

'But this does not explain why your family would write letters to him?' Maya asked.

'There's more to the story,' Ansh continued. 'I went off to Rajasthan. I rented a house in Jaisalmer and decided to travel to different villages from there. I wrote to Vivaan from there, and mentioned that I would be travelling. I was very excited about the way everything was turning out. But during my visit to Mokalsar, a small village, things took a nasty turn. I met an accident on the national highway...' Ansh completed.

'I was saved by a group of villagers, who took care of me and helped me recover. But I had lost a lot of blood by the time they found me. I was unconscious for almost two years. It's a very small village, and there I did not have any emergency contact information with me. I gained consciousness two days back, after which I went to Jaisalmer. I found piles of letters that Vivaan had written to me over this time. He wrote that my dad had passed away, that my family wanted to meet me, wanted me to come back. Vivaan received their letters because my sister knew that I was staying with Vivaan,' Ansh continued.

'But I don't understand why Vivaan wrote to your family?' Maya asked.

'After I stopped replying, Vivaan apparently came to Jaisalmer looking for me. But no one could tell him anything about me, as I hardly knew anyone there. I guess Vivaan didn't believe that I had simply disappeared, so he started to write to my family, keeping his hope alive. He also wrote to me, each month, asking me to come to Dehradun as soon as I receive his letters. So this morning, I went to Dehradun, to his house—your house. He hadn't bothered changing the locks over these 3 years. But everything seemed different. It had your presence all over, and I also found Tara's wedding invitation on the table; and I saw Vivaan's face looking at me through a garlanded picture frame. I have no idea, how

Vivaan left us, but I felt that perhaps it was time I came back to my family. After all, life indeed is short. But when Tara told me this morning that you were in my house, I felt all color drain out of my face. I felt that perhaps I could answer some of your questions and you could answer some of mine', Ansh said.

Maya felt the tears sting her eyes. Why hadn't Vivaan trusted her on this, and hadn't told her everything? However noble his purpose might have been, the fact that he had lied to her, pierced her heart each time she thought of it. She felt Ansh's eyes on her, and looked away. Her entire struggle over the past week to gather herself, to hold on, seems to have come crashing down. She didn't feel herself strong enough to answer him. How would she tell him that the guy she had fallen in love with, full of laughter and joy, had a part that she had been unable to reach out to? She somehow blamed herself for ~~Ansh~~ Vivaan's death.

If only… she had not walked away that morning after their fight, perhaps the three of them would be hanging out together, laughing over shared stories.

If Only…

She had stayed…

Age
Has several beautiful gifts,
But the one I could live without is pride.
Unforgiving. Unbending.
Developing a hardened exterior of being
    unreasonable.
Even as the child in us tries to reach out,
Through the tiny cracks in our skin,
A subtle gift that perhaps I could live without—
Giving me the power to love.
In all my childlike innocence

CHAPTER 8

Goodbyes

'Maya' Ansh's voice brought her back to the present. She saw Ansh looking at her, expecting her to say something. She told him that she met Vivaan six months back when she had moved to Dehradun. Things had been going very smoothly between both of them, but there seemed to be some enigma lurking behind Vivaan's happy exterior always. He would become very withdrawn at times, very distant. He had opened up to her eventually, yet she had somehow failed to notice the abyss that had driven Vivaan to jump off the cliff.

Maya felt that she had somehow failed to unravel the pain that had dwelled inside Vivaan. She wondered if she might have been able to convince him otherwise to not take his own life. If she hadn't walked out on him that afternoon, after another bout of anger and frustration that had hit him, if she had been with him when he had made up his mind that he didn't want to live anymore—Vivaan would still be there with them. Or if the letter had arrived earlier, she might have coaxed him to tell her about his past, his fears, and his insecurities.

But now that she knew the truth, Maya felt a strange tranquility settle in her heart. She had known 'Vivaan' as a man of principles, a loving human being; but today, she came to realize how great a friend he had been to Ansh. Giving his family support, even when there was no ray of hope. She felt a strange surge of respect and pride fill up in her heart. But his betrayal and inability to trust her entirely wrenched her heart.

It was almost 7 p.m. and she decided that there was nothing left for her in this town. She decided to go back to her home where Vivaan's memories awaited.

As she rose to leave, Ansh quietly added, 'Vivaan wrote about you Maya… How madly he was in love with you; how you inspired him, how you completed him… How he had started feeling a positive change in his life with you around. I wish this hadn't ended this way', he trailed off looking at Maya as the tears glistened in her eyes.

'Goodbye, Ansh', Maya said as she got into her car and she drove off.

A tiny sliver of change,
Embedded in her existence-
Each day, each moment – leads to her growth.
She evolves
Rising from the ashes of destruction,
Like a phoenix—
She soars high…
Over moon-glazed groves
Soaring into the night
Away from the probing eyes—
She finds her solace.

CHAPTER 9

Fighting the Oblivion

The next morning brought with it a heaviness that Maya had known to exist after she had lost her mother to cancer six years back. Maya had been living in United States working on her Ph.D. when the cancer was first diagnosed. Her mom's health had always been frail, and even after repeatedly telling her to visit the doctor, her mom had been negligent. By the time it was diagnosed, it was too late for a treatment.

Maya had taken a leave and spent the last few months with her mom. She had seen how the cancer spread deeper and gradually sucked out all life from her once vibrant and beautiful mother. Maya had been really close to her mother, and losing her was a pain that affected her so deeply that she felt something in her change. Her relationship with her father was no longer as vibrant as it used to be. They had just grown distant, with time. She had just come to accept the fact that people grow apart and not everyone we meet is supposed to stay in our lives forever. Maya had always believed that each person had a role to play, and when it was over, they left—one way or the other. But after her mother's demise, she no longer wanted to stay away from her own country.

When Maya was small, she always wanted to live in a place surrounded by hills and trees. Her search for peace brought her to Dehradun. And she felt it was the most wonderful decision of her. Else, how would she have met ~~Ansh~~ Vivaan? She wondered what Vivaan's purpose in her life was.

Yes. He had taught her to love again, love selflessly and fearlessly. His presence in her life had been like an elixir, fusing strength into her dying soul. But then why had she been unable to reach out to the darkness in his soul? Why had she been unable to offer the refuge to Vivaan that he had offered her?

Their relationship wasn't all silk and roses. They had their share of arguments and flaws. But both of them had been willing to work through them. Even the hardest fight they had strengthened their bond. And that was what she had loved the most about their relationship. Both of them had a willingness to change, to forgive, to grow and evolve. Both of them weren't too similar, but they loved their differences. Vivaan used to say to Maya that their combination completed each other.

Being in love with Vivaan had changed so much in her. She had felt herself evolve; yet his absence stung her existence. However logical she had been her entire life, losing the two people who meant so much to her had left her devastated. Each day, she felt just dragged onto the other, without any reason to survive.

How was she supposed to find a reason to live when her reason to wake up each morning had disappeared into oblivion?

Day by day
Breath by breath
Let the pillars of faith stand strong.
Often we try and resist changes,
Afraid of what lies on the other side of these
    changes.
Sometimes living through the changes—
Strengthens us.
Morphing our identity,
Honing our strengths.
Let us live embracing these changes,
Growing and evolving with them.
Gradually, slowly
And learning.
To live

CHAPTER 10

Getting It Back: Life

Ansh spent a long time sitting at the ghat, watching the serene water, after Maya had left. He and Vivaan often used to go there in the evenings. He and Vivaan had often visited the ghat together, sometimes to paint and write together—things that defined each of them. He never felt he would open up to any stranger the way he had to Maya. Perhaps that was why Vivaan had fallen in love with her. He wondered how different the situation would have been if he had been back to Dehradun a week before. He might have met Maya with Vivaan by her side. He never thought that someone was capable of loving a person so completely in a short span of time. But Maya had met Vivaan before six months. And the way her eyes seemed sad, told him that she had felt the loss no less than him. All he had wanted was to hold her close to him and cry. But the sheer oddity of the situation they were in stopped him from doing so.

It was almost ten at night when Ansh returned home. As soon as he entered, he saw the look of relief that passed between his mother and Tara.

'Oh, come on! I won't run away or something…' he said.

'You almost disappeared for three years', Tara quipped in.

'I am tired. Can you at least feed me, before you launch on to your lectures, Tara…' Ansh continued.

Tara and Ansh had always shared a playful relationship. They left no stone unturned to annoy the hell out of each other, but at the same time, they both adored each other. As they playfully made way to the dinner table, Ansh realized what a lot he had been missing out in his life since the past years. He missed having his family around him.

'Where is Maya? Isn't she coming back for the wedding?' his mother asked.

Ansh's hesitation didn't go unnoticed by Tara.

'Mom, there's a lot that you need to know. I don't know if she is coming back into this house again… I… I need to sort my mind before I can delve into the details…'

Later that night, as he lay in his bed looking up at the starry ceiling he had painted, Ansh thought back at the strange situation life had brought him to. He had never valued life, always being reckless and lived life at his own terms. When his father had tried to dissuade him from pursuing a career in painting, he had never even bothered to convince him otherwise, leaving his house and city without further thought.

Little had he known that it would cost him so much. His father and his best friend were simply erased from his life now. However hard he tried now, he wouldn't be able to bring them back. How he would have given everything in this world to talk to them again. His thoughts were a tangled mess of reasoning and what ifs when he finally fell asleep early next morning.

Life in death
Here comes fall—with its distinct naked branches,
Still holding onto a few traces of life.
The green of life,
Calling out against the dreary backdrop of death.
Though sad—masking the ultimate truth—
Of life thriving in harshest of conditions,
Slow, seething, undercover—but it stays.
The epitome of being
Of fights—against people, against conditions, and
    perhaps life itself.
Each moment seems difficult,
But nature hides life—
Even in death.

CHAPTER 11

The Void

Maya stirred in her sleep as the light morning breeze sent the curtains flying, and the sunlight streaked in. She opened one eye looking at the alarm clock that stood on the bedside table. It was still early morning, but Maya couldn't go back to sleep. As she lay carelessly on her back, she thought how the past six months had passed—uneventfully. After her encounter with Ansh, she had gradually tried to gather the broken pieces of her life. She had taken up a job at one of the local schools as an English teacher. After all the chaos and ordeal she had been through, teaching was something that brought peace to her life. When she interacted with the small children, she felt a new life stirred in her soul.

She still had two hours to get ready for school. Today, she was going to have a really busy day. The Diwali fundraising event for the local orphanage was almost a month away and she was in charge of the play that the children of sixth grade were about to perform. It was a dance drama on the life of prince Ram of Ayodhya: how he had been exiled for fourteen years, and later when he returned to his kingdom how the entire kingdom rejoiced—the essence of the festival Diwali to drive away darkness and welcome the light that existed within our soul—highlighted through the drama.

She had heard that every year this annual fundraiser was conducted at Dehradun since the past several years. It was a large-scale event where several people from different industries participated, and the funds were used to help the local orphanage to celebrate Diwali.

She got out of the bed finally, and decided to have a light breakfast before leaving for school. As she stood by the window with the cup of tea in her hands, she remembered how 'Vivaan' would sneak in behind her, holding her lightly in a warm embrace each morning. How he would slowly kiss under the hollow of her neck and mumble sweet nothings into her ears. She sighed as she thought that it was so unfair to have known love in the form she had, only to be taken away so soon—to be intoxicated with love knowing that it was never to come back again. She had made peace with the fact that Vivaan was gone forever, and that nothing could bring him back. She had perhaps forgiven him for the lies he had told her.

She had fallen in love with Vivaan's simplicity and his beautiful heart. She believed that even though the situation was dreary and difficult, Vivaan's love would always guide her with strength. As the birds started chirping, her train of thoughts finally broke away and she got ready to face another day in this dark world—where she was all alone, where Vivaan would not lift her up in his arms each time she squealed in excitement at having come across a new book; where Vivaan would not calm her down and make her go back to sleep after she woke up screaming after a nightmare.

Vivaan wouldn't be there—not anymore.

Life and its coincidences are elusive.
Making us meet new people,
People to whom we connect instantly,
Getting along
Like a house on fire—
Not knowing how those moments of resonance
Stay with us long after they have ceased to exist.
It is strange
How we search meanings in these moments—
Which are long lost,
But which refuse to leave our mind
Reminding us each moment of things
And people long left behind.

CHAPTER 12

Unanswered Questions

As Ansh gradually settled into his old life, he felt that he connected to his mother and Tara in a better way. Tara was getting married in less than a week, and with so much to do, he felt that he was consumed up by the sheer energy of the happiness it brought to their family. The guy Tara was getting married to, Shlok, was a decent fellow. He and Tara went to college together and had been in love for four years now. He felt so satisfied and happy realizing that his little sister was finally getting married.

The past few months had not been very easy for him. Finally, he had taken over his dad's business and helping his mother run them. The good thing was his mother was actively involved with different nonprofit organizations, helping orphan kids in any small ways that she could. She confessed to him once, that after his dad had passed away, she had lost all purpose in her life. It wasn't easy to be left behind by the person who meant the entire world to you. He wondered if Maya felt the same. Did she miss Vivaan so much? How was she coping up with her grief? Vivaan had never mentioned anything about her family in his letters, and he wondered if she was still in Dehradun.

Tara had coaxed him several times to call or visit Maya. But he didn't want to be an interruption to the gentle course her life might be taking. But there were times that he wished he could just talk to her... about Vivaan. Share with her all the memories that he had of their friendship. From what he had gathered from the time he had spoken to her, she didn't know anything of their friendship, of the small and stupid things they both had done for each other. Ansh wondered why Vivaan had not told Maya after all the ways he had loved her, and trusted her. He realized that perhaps it was his own insistence to not tell anyone about their 'deal' till he proved himself in front of his father. But what use was that now? Everything was under a state of chaos. He had no one to prove anything to anymore.

He wondered if he should invite Maya for Tara's wedding. But would she come if he did was the question that hovered in his mind.

Some days I feel you don't matter at all
Your absence would not sting me like the thorns of
    a rose briar
Nor would your presence fill me
With an ecstasy that would make my heart flutter
Some days I feel that the smile on your lips
    wouldn't bring one on mine
And yet you prove me wrong...
Hitting me with a spell of your being
Seeping in through my senses like the gentle
    whisper of the winds
Making me naive, vulnerable yet again
Oh memories, such havoc you create....
Nestled into my core
Questioning the core of my existence –
Yet again

CHAPTER 13

After You

Maya's life had developed a simple routine in the days that followed. She had allowed herself to be consumed up by her work and the preparations for the fundraiser event. It was interesting how her interaction with her students was actually helping her to get used with life again. Their joys and sorrows hovered around simple things, things that people sometimes overlook in the chaos of life.

She had found Vivaan's journals and had wanted to read through them. But she didn't feel that she was strong enough yet to go through his life just then. She felt that she needed some time to distance herself from everything his life had hovered around. She loved him too much to not be pulled into an abyss of unhappiness and sorrow of loss that still seemed fresh in her heart. Once when she had started reading, she stumbled across Ansh's name, and then she had shut the journal, purely because she still couldn't forget that Vivaan had not thought it fitting to share his life with her, and that was painful. How do you put into words one feels, that when you love someone in its entirety and yet there is a part of their soul that you cannot reach out to?

Recently, she had started writing again. It was something she and Vivaan had in common. They would often write stories together, parts of it, and later read it—cherishing the twists and turns their distinctly different writing styles infused onto it. Today was a Sunday and Maya had spent the entire day cleaning the house, re-arranging things around just so she would not have to think. She wanted to get so exhausted that she would fall asleep as soon as she hit the bed. It was still early evening when the doorbell rang. As she rushed to open the door, she tripped and fell. Maya was quite accident-prone and Vivaan often used to tell her that someday, when he isn't around, she surely would die in a simple accident.

Little did she know then that the irony would be on her fate?

When Maya opened the door, she found Tara beaming up to her. Maya couldn't help but smile.

'You look beautiful, Tara. The pre-wedding glow on your face is a telltale', Maya said before Tara could say anything.

'Come on in...' she completed.

Maya was well aware of Ansh being there, but she chose to ignore him. She somehow felt blaming him, for everything would rationalize Vivaan's actions to her.

'You have a beautiful house, I must say, Maya', Tara said, looking around.

'Thanks, Tara', Maya replied, still averting Ansh's gaze.

'So what brings you here? Anything I can help with?' Maya continued.

'Maya, I know you have had a difficult time... about everything... I just wanted to tell you, I really, really, want you to come to my wedding. Ansh told us everything... I am so sorry for everything.' And before Maya could respond, Tara came over and hugged her, holding her tightly in a warm embrace. The tears she had been holding back came un-bidding.

She realized that she had never longed so much for her mother than she had in the past six months. She literally had no one she could go to, to talk about things she was going through. Yes, she was healing, but it wasn't an easy process. There were times she felt like giving up everything and getting lost into oblivion herself. But Tara's warm gesture gave her a sort of assurance that she wasn't alone. That there were people like her, who were trying to deal with grief in their own ways.

When she pulled away, she saw tears in Tara's eyes.

'Vivaan was my friend as well. The three of us grew up together literally... I wish he hadn't taken this step...' Tara continued.

And so the three of them fell into a comfortable conversation talking about Vivaan and Ansh. It was almost ten at night when Ansh said that they had to leave. Maya looked outside and saw the overcast sky. It was probably going to rain through the night and asked them to stay overnight. Maya realized that driving back to Hardwar that late was probably not a very good idea.

'I will cook something and then we can chat. It's been months since I actually had a good conversation,' Maya said to Tara.

Ansh didn't feel too comfortable with the idea and wanted to leave, but Tara seemed to develop a fondness for Maya and she didn't want to go.

'I will call mom and tell her that we are staying here for the night. We can drive back early tomorrow,' Tara said.

And so it was decided.

What each of them was unaware of was storm that was gradually building up outside.

From the moment the seed of existence is sown,
Her presence is like the warm cave that provides
    refuge
To the wanderers lost in the biting cold.
Such is her love that even when miles separate us,
She knows when exactly I am not myself…
Needing support…
And above all, to restore the faith to believe in
    myself again.
None can rise above a mother's love they say…
The simplicity of forgetting all worries in her
    warmth is a feeling
Ingrained so deeply,
That even when she isn't nearby,
Her warmth stays.

CHAPTER 14

Deep Connections

The three of them stayed up late chatting. When they finally went to bed, it was one o'clock in the morning. Ansh had taken the couch in the living room. The loud banging of the windowpane woke up Maya. She remembered having closed all the windows before going to bed. She realized that perhaps the kitchen window had been left open. She groaned and got out of the bed where Tara lay asleep peacefully. She felt a peaceful connection with Tara. As she was heading back to the bedroom, she saw Ansh's silhouette by the window. She wondered if she should go and ask him, if he was just not sleepy, or if he needed something. He seemed lost in thoughts looking outside at the rain, which was beating down.

She went up slowly to him, so as not to startle him.

'Ansh? Do you need anything?' Maya asked.

Ansh didn't respond. Maya assumed he wanted to be left alone, and so she started to leave.

'There was this one time that Vivaan and me raced out in this storm just for a stupid bet we had placed between us', Ansh's voice reached out to her, stopping her midway. Maya suddenly realized that there was a lot about Vivaan she didn't know.

And both Maya and Ansh stood by the window talking about stupid stuff they had both done with Vivaan. Their moods lightened up with the happy memories, of the beauty of the moments that they had spent with their closest friend. They had so much to talk about suddenly that they didn't realize when the rain stopped and dawn crept up slowly. Maya felt relaxed and happy, in a long time she felt. It was the first time she felt that she had remembered Vivaan without getting sad. Tara and Ansh had brought in a kind of relief that she felt that she would have had if her mother were around.

They were still talking, when Tara walked into the room.

'I always love the mornings after it rains. It's so beautiful, fresh, crisp…' she said.

'I know. I love Dehradun more on mornings when it has rained the previous night. Freshen up. I will prepare tea and breakfast for us, and then you guys can leave whenever you want,' Maya said walking towards the kitchen.

Tara looked at her retreating form and said to Ansh, 'I really like her. Vivaan made a good choice.'

What she didn't hear was Ansh's silent murmur, 'I like her too…' as he got up and left the room.

'Remember me...
When I'm gone.
When I'm no longer there with you to walk along.
When we cannot walk together on sandy
      beaches...
And the world rushes on as everyone preaches.
Remember me
When in this mad world's race...
You are tired of hiding the tears that stain your
      face.
Remember me when you have to take a certain
      decision
But are torn apart—
Searching for precision.
Remember me.
On a cloudless night
When you see a lonely star...
And know for sure that in certain part of this vast
      creation
There is a heart that loves you deeply—
Know that I am your lifeline
That will pull you through
Rough waters and be there along—
During pleasant times
Remember me as the star that shine bright in the
      darkest night of your life
And you will find that happiness finds its way back
      to you—
Yet again.

CHAPTER 15

Going On

After Tara and Ansh left, Maya felt a weird kind of sadness. Perhaps it had been long that she had bonded with people so closely. She still had to get ready for school. The fundraiser event was closing in gradually and there was a lot to be done. She and her colleague Anaya had been working really hard over the dance drama and play, chalking out details of the decorations, dresses and other stuff.

Anaya was an easy person to be around. She never asked a lot of questions and mostly had so much to talk about that Maya didn't feel pressurized to talk around her. In fact, they had a comfortable camaraderie. There had been days when Maya would absolutely not want to talk to anyone, but with Anaya around, those days didn't feel so bad either. Coincidentally, Anaya was from Hardwar as well, and she wondered if she knew Vivaan, or perhaps Ansh. But she didn't want to ask Anaya in case she didn't. That would bring in a whole bout of questions, which she wanted to keep away from her workplace at any cost. She remembered Tara's insistence to attend her wedding and thought if she would. It would perhaps be a nice change to go and meet them sometime, she thought.

The rest of the week passed quite uneventfully, except for the fact that Tara had called her quite a few times and they had spent hours talking over the phone. Mostly it was Tara, discussing all her pre –wedding jitters with Maya. Maya felt like Tara was the younger sister she never had. In fact, she started looking forward to talking to her, sharing her life with Tara.

She thanked Vivaan that unintentionally he had brought in people to her life who understood her and shared her happiness or sorrows alike. Maya had learnt one thing in her life, that it's never easy to keep people in your life, but it was always great to have a few great friends. Getting attached to people had always been one of her weaknesses, but now she wasn't scared of being hurt. Her friendship with Tara wasn't based on any kind of expectation or need. It was just a simple bond, where two people respected each other and understood each other.

And she was thankful for this connection that had built up between the two of them.

The anxious heart
You don't follow any rules—
You don't know how to be pragmatic.
All you know is to beat
To the tunes of emotions guiding it.
And yet when the vein of reasoning gets strong,
It flutters and yet glows bright amidst the chaos of
*   being.*

CHAPTER 16

Knowing You

It had been a week since he and Tara had been back from Dehradun. But Ansh had been very distracted lately. Previously, whenever he was upset, he used to paint. But since he had come back, he did not feel like painting at all. Not once had he taken a look at the canvas that stayed in his room. But this morning, he had just felt so distracted and started sketching unintentionally. What he sketched were a pair of eyes, so deep in pain, so full of sorrow that he recognized immediately that they were Maya's eyes.

Tara's wedding was two days away and the amount of chaos in the house was unparalleled. Tara had grown very grumpy lately, and unreasonable at times. She would lock herself inside her room often, and rant about how no one cared for her wishes at her own wedding to Tara on phone. He didn't know how Maya convinced her, but when she would emerge from the room, she would be calm and understanding as if nothing had ever happened to spoil her mood in the first place.

Ansh at times felt envious of Tara. He still remembered how he and Maya had stayed up the entire night talking. Talking to her had been so easy, effortless. He had never felt so at ease with anyone, but then he knew that he couldn't afford to cross the fine line of distance that existed between them. As much as he liked her, she was in mourning for his best friend and he couldn't even think of letting her know of the turmoil in his head.

But perhaps she would be there at Tara's wedding. He felt a strange happiness that he knew had nothing to do with his sister getting married. Their mom had been busy recently with some event she was supposed to sponsor at some school, and so the entire responsibility of taking care of the wedding fell onto him. He and Vivaan had often annoyed Tara that at her wedding, they would make no stone unturned to burn the hell out of her, and that they would be happy to get rid of her in the long run. But Vivaan wasn't there anymore. His partner in crimes had chosen to walk out of their lives. It was difficult not to think of Vivaan frequently.

'Ansh…' Tara's voice wafted in through the door. He quickly crumpled the paper where he was sketching and threw it into the dustbin. He felt like a small kid who had been caught doing something he was not supposed to.

'Ansh, you need to take me for shopping today. I need to buy some stuff, and it's urgent,' she continued.

Ansh rolled his eyes, for he knew that for Tara, urgent could mean getting a pair of earrings. But he knew that it was her wedding and that he wanted to pamper her spoiled. After all, she was his only sister. He agreed to take here wherever she wanted, on the condition that she would make him a cup of tea before they leave.

'So where are we going exactly?' Ansh asked as he steered their car through the driveway of their house.

'I need to buy a lehenga. And matching earrings to go with it,' she continued.

'But I assumed that your shopping was done?' Ansh interjected. 'Mom made sure of that, didn't she?' he asked.

'It's for Maya,' she smiled looking into her phone.

What she didn't notice was the silence that accompanied them the entire time after she made this simple statement.

Dear friend
Perhaps words would never be enough to tell you
How your existence in my life is like sunshine—
Making my days bright, giving me the strength to
    face life.

Dear friend,
Perhaps words would never completely express to
    you
How each time I stumble and fall,
Your presence in my life gives me the courage to
    rise yet again.

Dear friend,
Sometimes your slight presence
Is all that I seek—
Ever so slightly the assurance
Of things to be alright…
So that even when you walk away
Your existence in me
Gives me the strength to hold on.

CHAPTER 17

The Wedding

Tara had asked Maya to come a day before the wedding, and so she was on her way to Hardwar again. Over the past few weeks, both of them had developed a close bond that both of them had come to cherish. As Maya stepped into their house, it seemed completely transformed with happiness, and with so many people around, that for a moment Maya felt that she had come to the wrong house.

But then she heard Tara scream, 'Maya...' and Tara came like a storm and swept her in an embrace. She had just gotten up the dry mehndi off her hands and she showed off the beautiful design on her hands and feet to Maya.

'Come on, I have so much to talk about. I am so excited and so nervous at the same time. I am glad you could come today', Tara said, taking Maya to her room. Maya had written a letter for Tara as her wedding gift and bought a pair of traditional earrings for her as well. The look on Tara's face was priceless when she saw the gifts and she became teary eyed.

'I got something for you too… And you will be wearing this at my wedding', Tara said, pointing to the light pink and floral patterned lehenga that lay on the bed.

'I… I…' Maya started to say. But the dejection on Tara's face stopped her. She said instead, 'It's beautiful… I will absolutely wear it tomorrow.'

They got busy chatting and talking about so many things. Maya was wondering where Tara's mom and Ansh were when he stepped in to check if Tara needed something. He seemed surprised to find her there.

The next morning, as Tara got ready for the day, she didn't seem like her usual chirpy self. Maya sensed her silence and asked her if she was okay. Tara was teary eyed and said, 'I feel so drained suddenly. I had been waiting for this day for so long and now that it is here, I feel strange. I miss my dad…', she said.

Maya didn't know what to say to that. She reached out and held Tara's hand, and told her that, 'In life we can't always have people whom we love dearly, to be around always. There would be times that they won't be there, that you would have to be alone. But that doesn't mean that they don't love you anymore. They are just not around to tell you that. And count your blessings—your mom, Ansh, all of us are here. Just know that wherever your dad is, he is happy for you.'

Tara finally smiled, 'You are right, Maya. You are such a great friend. I wish we had met before.'

Oblivious to both of them, Ansh—who's standing outside their room—thought the same.

Sometimes light that shine bright
Are like an illusion,
Of dreams,
Of beautiful things,
Of thoughts that propel us towards positivity.
Be the light that shines,
Through darkness, and stands out
As a hope—
Hope that doesn't know how to lay dormant.
It keeps your soul awake—bright and happy.
Searching, smiling and wanting more—
Illuminating your soul.

CHAPTER 18

Connections of the Soul: Ansh

Tara looked ravishing in her golden colored sari. As she walked down the stairs, towards a new dawn of her life, a new journey with the person she loved, Tara looked like an angel. Looking at her filled Ansh with a strange surge of happiness. Over all these years, when he had missed being away from his family, he had never realized how being there together through happy and sad moments mattered. He wished that his dad was around—he would have been so happy to see their little princess all grown up. Ansh could sense that his mother was a little sad, that Tara would be soon shifting to a new place, away from them.

And then walking beside Tara was Maya. She was wearing the dress Tara had chosen for her. It was difficult for him to not stare at her—her beauty lay in her simplicity and her smile. He felt that her smile could calm all storms—that was the effect she was beginning to have on him. How he wished that Vivaan were around. The crazy banter around died down soon, as the wedding rituals proceeded. And before he realized Tara was married off to the person of her dreams. Shlok was a nice fellow and Ansh really liked him. He felt that Tara would be happy.

All the rituals took a long time to finish and by the time the guests had left, it was well past midnight. A strange heaviness enveloped him, which he knew had nothing to do with just his sister leaving. He knew that Maya would leave early next morning. After the long day of exhaustion, he wanted nothing more than to settle down with a cup of coffee at his favorite spot at the terrace, doing nothing. He knew, had Vivaan been around, both of them would have sneaked out late, making up some random plan. Heading towards his room, he found Maya standing by the window looking outside. She seemed to be lost deep in thoughts. Ansh had an urge to go and talk to her. He wanted to talk to her, about everything and about nothing at the same time. He found it difficult how this stranger was gradually tugging at his heart. He hesitated for a moment, before knocking at her door.

When she turned to look at him, her face tired and exhausted, she almost looked angelic. And then there was her smile. He wondered how each time her smile seemed so refreshing, as if nothing in the world could ever bother her. Perhaps she knew magic.

'Ansh', Maya shook him.

He didn't realize he had been lost in his own thoughts.

'Sorry, I think I blanked out for a moment', he laughed.

'For complete five minutes. So, how do you feel? Tara seemed so happy. I am really happy for her,' Maya continued.

'Yes. She is really happy. I don't know exactly how I feel. I have lost two important people who meant a lot to me, and even now the pain of separation is too much to bear. I guess our vulnerabilities make us humans,' Ansh said.

'True. I don't know if we can ever get used to the fact of people close to our heart—not being there. That they no longer exist,' said Maya.

As their conversation continued, it was not mere attraction that pulled him towards Maya. It was perhaps the awareness of loss that bound them together.

That and Vivaan.

Chapter 19

Connections of the Soul: Maya

As Maya was getting ready to leave the next morning, Tara barged in, all happy and excited.

'Maya…' she screamed, 'I can't believe that I am married now.'

Her childlike enthusiasm was contagious, and Maya smiled. She felt so connected to Tara, and loved her like a long lost sister.

'Being married, suits you though', said Maya. 'I am glad that I came to your wedding, it was so much fun. I felt like I was among my own family,' she continued, hugging Tara.

'I am glad you could make it. You are like family to us. By the way when are you planning to leave for Dehradun?' Asked Tara.

'Well, soon. I am almost done packing', Maya said pointing at the bag she was packing.

'Well, mom is really sad that I am leaving. Ansh doesn't care though.' Tara continued.

Maya pointed out that he might be more affected than he is letting her realize, perhaps. After all, she was his only sister.

Tara eyed Maya suspiciously, which made her a little uncomfortable.

'So you are his new friend or what, that he shared his sorrows with you?' laughed Tara.

Maya started laughing, too, at the assumptions Tara was making.

As it was time for her to leave, she felt sad. She knew that in the short span she had known Tara and Ansh, they had become really good friends—people whom she could well call as her family. People who knew wouldn't judge her, or the choices she would make in her life. It was this comfort, this connection that had helped her settle down gradually.

After Vivaan.

And then there was Ansh. Lately, she had started feeling comfortable talking to him as well. He and Vivaan might have been friends, but they were not too much alike. While Vivaan had won her over by his childlike enthusiasm, his stupid jokes and his writing, no doubt Ansh's presence offered her a strange calm. She had later realized that the room she had first stayed in belonged to Ansh and the fact that he had painted the ceiling himself made her admire him. She really felt that he was as talented a painter as Vivaan was as a writer. She wondered if he would paint again. She really felt that he should. But more than that, she felt a connection with him.

Perhaps it was the knowledge that they both loved the same person in a way that was untainted by any form of envy that seemed to connect them.

A connection that felt deep.

A connection that was real.

Between the abyss of darkness,
And the open sky of brightness,
There lies the finest line of difference—
Keep looking into the darkness
And the wild glow of the burning lamp will be
    missed.
We keep looking on at the wrong places, perhaps
A little more of sunshine in our hearts
And you emerge a winner

CHAPTER 20

The Fundraiser

Life had started rolling once again for Maya after Tara's wedding. All her time nowadays was being taken up for the preparation of the Diwali event.

With the fundraiser event only a few hours away, Maya could feel the energy and the rhythm that had engulfed the entire school. It had been a busy morning, with the stage rehearsals, decorations, and the preparations for the evening keep everyone on their toes. For Maya, this wasn't simply a fundraiser event. She had given her heart and soul into this event, wanting it to become successful. It had sort of become like an elixir for her soul, the only part of her existence that she looked at with joy in her heart. She had been made the event coordinator and had taken up the task very seriously. Every year, the event was graced by the presence of a local politician; but this year, on Maya's insistence, the school authorities had requested a renowned social worker, Mrs. Raheja, to be the Chief Guest. Maya had heard from her friends at the local library that Mrs. Raheja worked closely with various organizations to secure funds for the different orphanages. Even without meeting her, Maya had developed a strange respect for this woman, who had a mission in her life, where she actually had tried and made a difference in the lives of several people.

Maya checked the stage one last time, before she decided to go and get ready for the event. Even though she had no desire to get dressed up for the event, being the coordinator, she felt it would be suitable if she donned some traditional attire. When Vivaan was in her life, she never took the trouble of spending hours deciding what to wear. He always told her what would look nice, and she loved whatever he chose for her. But today, she had a task at hand. She couldn't believe that the existence of a single person depended so much on another. The closeness of the human ties and the complexities of the emotions amazed her. How smoothly people blend into our lives and once they leave, it seems unbearable to be able to survive without them.

She had spent the last 30 minutes looking at her wardrobe, thinking of what to wear. She looked at the clock and panicked—she had exactly an hour left to get ready. She hastily chose a golden colored sari. This one had always been her favorite—a hand me down from her mother. As she touched the sheer fabric, a strange longing rose in her heart, a need to talk to her mother. It had been so long that she hadn't spoken to her family, let alone told them what all she had gone through in the past few months. The inability to reach out to her family spread like a venom in her heart. She had tried hard to stay connected with her father, but perhaps he had got too busy in the daily chores of his married life.

She chose a pair of simple earrings to wear with her golden colored sari. This pair had been Vivaan's favorite. She hastily dressed up, and decided to avoid wearing any makeup, except for the kohl that she always applied on her eyes. Vivaan used to joke she looked like a ghost early in the morning on the days that she forgot to remove the kohl before bed.

Vivaan—she sighed again. This is an important day for us, she thought. She wished that he had been there to accompany her to this event, his presence would have made all the difference, she thought as she left the house. As she reached the venue, the entire ambience seemed electrified. Everyone was dressed up, the women showing off their expensive dresses and jewelry, the kids running about in ecstasy. As the event started, a hush fell over the hall. Maya could feel her heart racing as the time for the play drew nearer. She wished good luck to the performers and stood backstage, eager to see how it goes. She felt pride surge in her heart as the children performed to the best of their abilities. She had never felt so satiated, so happy.

When the play was over, the Chief Guest, Mrs. Raheja, came on stage to address the audience. She spoke words of encouragement and appreciation for the way the event had been organized. She was not surprised to see that it was Tara's mom. She felt foolish at not having made the connection earlier. Tara's mother had been an active social worker, she knew that. She made it a point to meet her after the event and asked her about Tara—how she was coping up with her new life. Tara had been married for almost a week now, and she hadn't been able to get in touch with Tara yet.

A sumptuous fete followed the event, where different food stalls had been set up to further aid the fund raising aspect of the entire event. She was talking to Anaya about how the children had done a great job and made the event a successful one. It was already quite late and Maya was wondering if it was time to leave now. The day had been so tiring that she felt a wave of exhaustion sweep over her.

Anaya wanted her to stay for some more time, and said they could go back together. But now that the event was over, Maya felt an emptiness growing inside her. She felt she needed some solitude and a warm cup of tea to calm herself down. After promising Anaya to meet her for lunch the next day at the school cafeteria, she rushed out to avoid being stopped for some conversation by some other people of the school. After all, everyone had worked so hard for this day and now was the time to relish and enjoy the success of the event. She felt that she would call Tara sometime later that week, and decided to leave.

As she reached her car and was fumbling inside her bag looking for her car keys, she heard someone call out to her. The dim lighting in the parking lot made it difficult for her to see and identify who had called out. As he came nearer, Maya froze. Ansh was walking towards her. Why hadn't she thought he might be there with his mom? Maya seemed to be at a loss, at how she should react. The last time she had met him at Tara's wedding, both of them had been very emotional. They had avoided talking much because of a silent agreement between them that their conversation might open up wounds both of them were trying to shield.

'Oh! Vivaan', she thought. 'How am I supposed to move on after you if people from your past keep appearing in like ghosts all of a sudden in my life?'

Through the endless void
Of the unknown—here I am.
Discovering myself
Even as you left a deep void in my soul.
I am discovering myself—
In the small sips of the tea from my favorite but
worn out cup.
I am discovering myself—
Yet again in the fresh feel of the rain against my
naked skin.
In the petrichor of the first shower that threatens
to draw me into the depths of memories.
I am discovering myself—
Amidst the musty smell of old leather bound
books.
Yes, I will find myself.
Even in the void you left behind.

CHAPTER 21

Lifelines

'Hi Ansh', said Maya.

'Hi, Maya. It's been quite long. I did not expect you to meet you here... at this event. So, how are you? How's life going on... after... the last time we met?' mumbled Ansh.

'It's ok, Ansh. I guess we both are trying to move on from where we left. I teach at this school. So what are you up to these days? Did Tara settle down well in New York? I haven't been in touch with her lately', said Maya.

'Well, everyone is fine. She has settled down but with the time difference, it's difficult to keep track of people. She's still settling in. She keeps asking about you... As for me, I am busy handling dad's business as for now,' continued Ansh.

Maya remembered that she still needed to call her father and talk to him.

'I think I will leave for home now. I had a long day. By the way, if you are in Dehradun sometime, come to my house. The last time when Tara was around we had a great time', Maya said getting into her car.

'Sure thing. Take care, Maya,' Ansh replied.

As she drove away, she saw Ansh's silhouette getting fainter in the rearview mirror. She sighed thinking about the strange turn of events the night had witnessed. When she had left for the event earlier that evening, she had no idea that she would come face to face with Ansh again. It was a strange feeling that she had come to love the name Ansh because of the person it was associated with in her life. But look at life, the moment we feel that we have learnt all its secrets, it reveals to us a new facet, something completely unknown to us. Maya stifled a yawn as she parked the car in front of her house, and let herself in. She decided to go to bed without further ado, and freshened up. As she changed into her sleeping gown, her cell phone beeped. She looked at her bedside clock that read 11.30 p.m. She felt strange that someone would text her this late at night, and wondered if she should bother checking her phone. Her head throbbed with pain and her eyelids grew heavy with sleep. The sleep got better of her, and she decided to check her cellphone the next morning and went to bed.

Maya woke up to the banging of her windowpanes. At first, she was confused at the bright lights that suddenly seemed to fill up her entire room. Then she realized that a storm was raging outside. By the time she closed all the windows and got into bed again, she was wide awake. She lay there, tossing and turning, trying to get back to sleep, but then she simply couldn't sleep. It was one in the morning and she cursed the weather outside for waking her up. She scooped up her cell phone and found two new text messages from an unknown number.

'Hi, Maya. Hope you reached home safely. Ansh here.'—
it read. This was the first time Ansh had texted her.

Maya felt a sudden void inside her. She had first met
'Vivaan' in Dehradun when she had gone to a bookstore
and she was searching for a copy of *Great Expectations*
in the classic section. This book had been real close to
her heart since she was very small, and often she would
read it over and over again. But amidst her busy life, she
seemed to have misplaced her copy and wanted to get a
new one—a hardbound, glossy leather-bound edition this
time. Coincidentally, the only edition the store had, was
being taken away by the tall guy in the black t-shirt she
saw. He had a pile of books held out in front of him. She
wondered if he planned to buy all of those, or would sort
out a few favorites. She decided to wait and see if the brown
leather bound edition of *Great Expectations* had any scope
of being left behind. With this in mind, she started following
him around the store. The pile of books in his arms kept
on growing to the point that he had to transfer them to a
cart. Maya was fascinated. Being a book lover, she always
found herself melting away to people who loved books. She
realized that there was a slim chance that this person would
be planning to filter away the copy of *Great Expectations*,
which was a collector's edition. So she decided that she
would perhaps come back later, and turned away. She went
to look at some of the other classics, thinking she would
get something worth reading. She was busy checking out
some books by Charles Dickens when she almost collided
with someone. It was the guy in the black t-shirt who had
stolen away her book, she felt. She excused herself when he
asked her, 'Do you always follow strangers around, or is it
just the bookstore that fascinated you today?' his eye full
of laughter.

Maya felt embarrassed and said, 'Actually, I was hoping that you would decide not to buy one of the books from the pile you collected, and so I was just following that book. I am sorry to appear like a stalker, but I had absolutely no intentions of following you.'

'So which one was it?' he said.

'Great Expectations', Maya replied.

'Oh! You can keep it. I have read *Great Expectations* already and was planning to buy it for a friend of mine. He is not that much of a reader. So he won't mind', he replied.

Maya felt reluctant, yet a part of her grew very happy at this serendipity. She tried to keep a straight face and said, 'Are you sure you won't mind if I buy that book? It's a collector's edition after all...'

The guy in the black t-shirt smiled and said, 'Well you can compensate for my loss by having a cup of coffee with me.'

And that was how it started their friendship. He had told her later that her name was Ansh and that he worked as a freelance writer.

'Hi, Maya. Hope you reached home safely. I really had a great time talking to you. Ansh here.' This was exactly what Vivaan had texted after she had reached home.

The fact that Ansh—the real one—had texted her brought back not only memories, but also immense pain. The happy moments that she had shared with him made her realize that the void that his absence had created would last forever. She could perhaps replace the number in her contact list, but she wondered if replacing someone's memories was an easy task. Maya wondered if she should reply or just let the past rest as it is. But Vivaan was not a part of her past that she wanted to forget. He was a part of memories that she knew she would cherish forever. She felt that there was so much that she still had to know about him, things that if they had stayed together would have revealed themselves to her in due course of life. Curiosity got the better of her and she felt that perhaps Ansh could tell her a lot more about Vivaan.

'Thanks, Ansh. I reached safely,' Maya wrote.

The cell phone beeped almost instantly.

Ansh: Still awake?

Maya: The storm doesn't help me to sleep.

Ansh: Outside, or in your head?

Maya: Perhaps both.

Ansh: The ghosts won't let me sleep either.

Maya: Hmm.

Ansh: Am I allowed to talk to you about Vivaan?

Maya: Yes. I wanted to ask the same. Can I?

Ansh: Yes, of course.

Maya: I miss him so much. At times I feel that someone has cut off my oxygen supply and forced me to into the deep ocean...

Ansh: I know how it feels. He was my best friend. In fact the only person whom I could fall back on irrespective of any situation. I miss him too.

Ansh: I am leaving tomorrow and will be back at Dehradun next week. Do you want to meet? I think sometimes it's good to have people around you, with whom you can talk and share your pain with.

Maya: I will think about it. Right now, there's too much in my head to stay clear. Goodnight. I am sleepy.

Ansh: Goodnight, Maya. Sleep well.

Maya did not feel that she was completely ready for this. Meeting Ansh to talk about Vivaan was not going to be easy for her. Perhaps it was not going to be easy for Ansh as well. But Ansh did not have to wince each time he mentioned Vivaan. Ansh could not feel the pain that both his and Vivaan's name inflicted on her. She had forgiven them for the lies, but still the pain remained. Talking to Ansh had been easier than she had thought, perhaps because both of them were familiar to the pain of losing someone really close to their heart. She had heard that pain brings people closer, but today she felt that this pain was becoming like a lifeline to her sustenance now.

Lifelines.

It was the last thought she had before she fell back deep into slumber.

There you stand
Hovering at the brink of my consciousness,
Like a half forgotten melody—
Escaping me each time I make an effort to
*   remember and spell it out by words.*
There you are
Like pure magic,
The story that I have always wanted to write—
Set amidst exotic places
Exuding the vibrancy of my imagination.
There you are
In all your simplicity—
Ethereal, and magical
Like stardust
Asking me to let go and follow the only thing that
*   matters...*
My heart

CHAPTER 22

Stardust

The storm had subsided by the time Maya woke up the next morning. There was a soothing calmness in the air. The rains had cast a haze of chill over the city and it almost transformed it. The leaves appeared a distinct shade of bright green, as if they had burst forth from a bud reflecting a new life overnight. The sky was clear and distinct, with its azure color casting everything in a merry light. Maya remembered that she had promised Anaya to meet at the school cafeteria for lunch. The thought brought a smile to her lips. Maya always found it easy to talk to Anaya, with her cheerful voice lifting up her spirits. Maya decided to cook some flattened puffed rice—'poha'—for lunch because she knew how much Anaya loved this recipe. Maya had found a dear friend in Anaya at her workplace and she loved to cook for her at times.

Maya called her father on her way to school. He seemed mildly surprised that she had called so early in the day. Usually, Maya used to call him on the days when there was something special—either a festival or some anniversary—but she knew very well that he was past the point of caring. Maya felt relieved after listening to his constant complaints that she had not visited them for quite some time. She finally hung up after promising that she would visit them the next month. Maya had to teach three classes that morning, before she would meet Anaya. The day was passing uneventfully. It was one of those days that seemed to drag on without any special purpose or accomplishments. As the bell for the recess chimed, Maya headed towards the cafeteria. She found Anaya waving at her from a corner table.

'Hi! Maya, did you get poha this time?' was the first thing that Anaya asked, even before Maya could settle down. Anaya's childlike enthusiasm pleased Maya.

'Yes, I did. And I made it extra spicy, just the way you like it', winked Maya.

'By the way, are you free next Friday? It's my daughter Rhea's first birthday and we are having a small gathering at my house. Some close friends of Rahul and mine would be there, and Rhea's friends from the playschool. It would be a lot of fun if you can make it', said Anaya.

'You already know that I don't have much to do after school. It sounds like a great idea. Let me know if you need help with the preparations. Anything at all that I can help with', replied Maya.

'I didn't recognize that Mrs. Raheja was Ansh's mom', she said to Anaya.

At the mention of his name, Anaya nodded and grew silent. But the silence didn't last for long. The lunch passed in their crazy banter, talking about all the stuff that Anaya still had to take care of for the party, cracking jokes about how the Principal, Mr. Aggarwal, looked on through from the top of his fat rimmed glasses to give the students a stern look but ended up looking funny. They headed towards their respective classes after lunch, promising to keep in touch over the next week. Diwali was two weeks away and the school would be closing for the Diwali vacations for a week. This was a crazy time of the year, as the semi-annual exams were scheduled soon after the school re-opened, giving the teachers a tight deadline to complete their syllabus and prepare the students for the exams.

Maya had covered almost all the chapters that she was supposed to teach before the vacations, yet she wanted to give ample questions to the students beforehand so that they were well prepared for the exams.

Ever since she was young, Maya had dreamt of becoming a teacher. She felt, if she could bring about a positive change in life of even one of her students, it would serve her purpose. And being able to interact closely with the children gave her hope, infused a positive energy in her that helped her to go on. She was happy that she had found this job. This, in fact, was more than a job to her—she felt it was her bridge to her existence. When Maya went back home after school, she found herself in a dismal mood. She thought of writing something on her blog to take her mind off the restlessness that she had been feeling. But she felt so distracted that even writing down something seemed impossible to her at this point.

She decided that she would go for a walk in the park close to her house that evening. The emptiness in her heart had nothing to do with school getting over, she knew. She did not want to let herself think about Vivaan; she knew that if she gave in to the temptation of the thoughts, then the abyss of hopelessness and memories would consume her, not giving her any path to escape. And with Vivaan, uninvited thought of Ansh came. Over the last two meetings with him, she found herself melting towards this stranger, just because he was associated with the name that had meant the world to her. At times, Maya wondered if she would ever be able to warm up to any other person as easily as she had with Vivaan. She still found it strange to refer to him as Vivaan, and this brought an uninvited pain in her heart.

Over the next few days, Maya got was swept away by the sudden load of work that came prior to closing of the school. Anaya had asked her for some help to get her house ready for Rhea's party on Friday evening. It was decided that they would leave for Anaya's house soon after school that day and take care of everything that needed to be done. Anaya was quite excited about the entire situation. It was the first time that she was actually planning a party for Rhea, and even though Rhea was quite young to understand, Anaya wanted everything to be perfect for her tiny princess. Maya and Anaya spent the entire Friday afternoon getting the hall ready for the birthday party. Balloons, streamers, paper cuttings cluttered the entire room. By the time it was 6 p.m. they had everything in order.

Even Rhea seemed excited and happy and jumped around the entire room, her eyes shining with excitement. Anaya had baked the chocolate and cream cake herself. Rahul was busy taking care of the guests who had started to arrive. Holding Rhea by her hand, Anaya looked ravishing in her deep blue sari. Maya felt warmth fill up in her heart looking at them together. Maya had chosen a simple white colored full sleeved *kurta* and had paired it up with blue jeans, her favorite combination of colors. After the cake cutting was over, the children got busy playing games. Maya, holding a glass of wine in her hand, headed outside towards the porch and sat down on the wooden swing overlooking the small garden. From here, Maya could get a complete view of the ongoing party, but it gave her the seclusion that she seeked at the point. She did not want to hurt Anaya's emotions by being a spoilsport at the party, so she decided to stay here for some time, by herself. She sat looking at the night sky that seemed like a vast sepulcher of the glittering stars. When she was young Maya often thought that someday she would spend her nights awake looking up at the sky.

'Wonderful, isn't it?' his voice chimed in.

Maya found Ansh standing beside her, looking up at the sky in awe that was a reflection of her own. She remembered that Ansh had told her that Anaya was a friend of his. Why hadn't she thought before that he might be here too?

'Mmmm...' Maya replied, taking a sip of the wine.

'Did I disturb you?' Ansh asked.

'No. I was just... thinking. So when did you come to Dehradun?' asked Maya.

'Yesterday. I tried not to come here today, but Anaya wouldn't listen. She made Rahul call me three times since morning so that I would give in. But I am glad I came. It's a nice party', Ansh said.

'Yes. It is full of life and laughter. I wish our lives could be this beautiful', Maya felt a little lightheaded. Maya wanted to go back to her house and just sleep.

'I am not feeling too well. I think I will tell Anaya and head back home', Maya said.

'Did you drive here?' asked Ansh.

'No, I actually walked. It's not too far from the school', replied Maya.

'I am planning to go back as well. Do you mind if I walk you home?' asked Ansh.

Maya hesitated for a moment before saying 'No'.

By the time Ansh and Maya said their byes to Anaya and Rahul, most of the guests had already left.

As they left together Anaya looked at Rahul and asked, 'Do you think that something is brewing between them? Maya is always so silent, I don't even know if I should ask her anything yet?'

'Let them be. Certain things are like stardust. The moment you try to hold onto them, they disappear.'

Just like stardust.

These thoughts,
These words—
Made up of a million delicate emotions
Like the paper-thin wings of a butterfly...
It's magical how these words carry a heavy
    burden
The weight of happiness expressed...
The strength borne by its inspirations...
And above all the weight of things
Left unsaid...

CHAPTER 23

Unending Storms

Maya's house was a 20-minute walk from Anaya's house. As Maya and Ansh walked side by side, none of them seemed to notice the silence that had settled in between them. Perhaps both of them were grateful for it. Suddenly, Ansh sighed and said, 'I wish that this situation was different. I wish Vivaan were here today. He was my only close friend. My life has been such a roller coaster ride since the past three years, that now I would give anything in the world to bring the people I lost back in my life again. I miss him so much.'

'Vivaan was so full of life. It's kind of ironical that in his last days he was at the mercy of life. I sometimes wonder how it would be to know him for years together. I envy you, Ansh, you have so many years to look back to, and I have just few months, to know and love this wonderful person', Maya's voice cracked.

She gave Ansh a tired smile. Without thinking, Ansh reached out for her, touched her face gently and said, 'Life is not always fair, you see.' As the tears glistened in her eyes,

Maya's pain called out to him and Ansh couldn't turn away. He took her in his arms, soothing her as if she was a small child who needed to be comforted after a nightmare. 'It's okay, Maya…'

When she finally drew back and looked at Ansh, his eyes were filled with tears too. At that moment Maya felt she could feel the pain that Ansh felt, at having lost his best friend. His grief pulled at her, mingled somewhere in the darkness with her own pain. She wanted to tell him that it would all be okay and that he would survive, that they both would make it through this loss, but the words wouldn't come.

Ansh gazed at her and she knew he was seeing her through the haze of his tears. He touched her cheek; his hand slid down to coil around her neck and pulled her close. She knew that this moment would last forever, as a memory, even when she would want to forget it. Perhaps she would wonder what had affected her so, whether it was the wine or the cool breeze that made her want to forget all sense of time and space. Or perhaps the loneliness that lay deep in her soul, trying to break free. She whispered his name softly—Ansh—in the darkness. The kiss she placed on his cheek was meant to comfort him, of that she was sure. But when he turned his face towards her and their lips touched, soft and pliant and salty with teardrops, something changed.

The kiss turned passionate and desperate. What mattered at that moment was their being together. The cool night air seemed to caress their skins. In some part of her mind, Maya knew that she was being carried away, but it felt so good. With a groan, she pulled away. Ansh buried his face in his hands. 'This didn't happen', Maya whispered in an uncertain voice. She refused to look at him.

'Maya…' Ansh said unsteadily.

'I need to go, Ansh', said Maya and rushed away, leaving Ansh standing on the road.

Long after she had left, Ansh started walking back towards his house, a storm raging in between his heart and mind.

The moment of departure spells
I'll miss you,
But it's more
The feeling of leaving behind—people, places,
Leaving behind moments that saw you,
Celebrated you,
And let you go.
As you depart,
You leave behind a part of you
That will never be the same again.
Is it this knowing
That brings the feeling of Tosca?
A longing,
And you keep drifting
Into the memories of moments
That you long left behind.

CHAPTER 24

The Retreat

As Maya stepped inside her house, she stumbled on to her bed and sat there. Tears stung her eyes. It had been six months since Vivaan had gone, and tonight she had broken her vows to the man she loved; she felt that she had shattered the faith she'd made to love Vivaan till the day she would die. She felt ashamed and guilty. She wanted to call Tara and tell her what had happened. And then there was Ansh; she wondered why hadn't he stopped. 'Was he carried away too? Carried away by the emotional turn of events? What would he be thinking of her?' she thought. Her head was so heavy that she felt it would explode. She decided that she would go to bed and not think of what had happened that night ever again.

Ansh lay awake in his bed, thinking of what had happened between him and Maya that night. He felt tightness in his chest, at perhaps having betrayed his best friend. It was true that even before he had met Maya, the way Vivaan had written about Maya, it was easy to fall in love with the beautiful heart that he had described she possessed. But each time he met Maya, he had felt a storm raging inside in his heart. Each time he decide that he would keep away from her, but then her deep eyes that were so sad, seemed to pull him towards her. Tonight, when he saw her sitting on the porch with a glass of wine looking up at the stars, he couldn't stop himself from going to talk to her. He wanted to know what thoughts hovered at the brink of her consciousness; he wondered what it would be to listen to those lips talk to him. Talk about anything and everything that mattered, and even stuff that did not matter.

But he knew that tonight they had crossed the line—he had crossed the line and that perhaps both of them would never be able to forgive themselves for whatever had happened. Vivaan was like a brother to him and he felt that he had broken the line of trust that had been placed between them ever since they were young. But it was so easy to talk to Maya, without any inhibitions, without the worry of what she would think. Ever since Ansh had been back, he felt this strange disconnect with all the people he had been once known. Perhaps the pain had brought about a change in him—a change so strong and deep that he could no longer go back to the person he once used to be, before everything changed. These thoughts troubled him and wouldn't let him sleep. He tossed and turned in his bed, and wondered if he should text Maya. Maybe apologize to her so that she wouldn't feel uncomfortable around him the next time they met. Or perhaps it would be better if they did not meet again.

With these thoughts in mind, he finally fell asleep. When Ansh woke up the next morning, the sun was still not high up in the sky. The faint pink light in the sky was the remnant of the deep inky night before. The lingering discomfort he felt reminded him of whatever had happened the night before. He knew that his next meetings were scheduled not before Monday, and it was only Saturday yet. He wondered if he should leave for home the same day. He felt that if he stayed on in Dehradun for another day, he would find himself knocking on Maya's door.

But what he wasn't still sure of was how would he face her, let alone talk to her. He groaned and got off the bed. He decided to go for a run. Dehradun in the morning was a beautiful sight, with its green trees and curved roads, and spelled a sight right out of a post card. The small roadside teashops would be getting ready for the day. Ansh took in the smell of the fresh morning and the faint spices that wafted through the air, as the small teashop owners got ready for the early morning tea to be served to the customers, most of whom were people who had gone out early for a morning walk and stopped by to relish a cup of tea. He remembered how he and Vivaan would often stay awake into the wee hours of the morning sometimes talking, sometimes working, and sometimes watching stupid old movies, and then would go for a cup of tea early morning.

He missed Vivaan more than he would allow himself to admit. Whenever he talked to Maya, he felt that a faint connection with his childhood friend still remained and he felt like holding onto her like a lifeline, like an anchor. But he did not want to make things difficult for Maya at the same time. He knew that it was still difficult for her to refer to him as Ansh; he could see it in her eyes. Ansh decided he would get some groceries before going back. The nearest supermarket was a few blocks away from where he was staying. In his mind, he made a list of stuff he would need for the weekend—some fruits and snacks and headed towards the supermarket. As he moved along the aisles of fruits and other stuff he needed, he spotted Anaya with Rhea. He headed over to them and played a bit with Rhea. She was still sleepy in Anaya's arms but her eyes brightened up as she saw Ansh. Even though Anaya had been dating Ansh before he left for Rajasthan, they had fallen out of touch with time. But now Ansh somehow felt it was easier talking to people who didn't seem too attached to him. It gave him a sense of security and freedom- that he didn't need to talk about his past to them. Anaya turned and waved at someone behind him, and he turned to find Maya walking towards them.

A shiver ran through his insides, as he remembered the softness of her lips that he had kissed the night before, and then came the uninvited thought of the tears in her eyes as she had walked away from him. Without waiting for another moment, he pretended to pick up a call on his cell phone, wished a quick bye to Anaya and Rhea and walked away. With each step he took he could feel Maya's eyes bore into his back.

It took all his resolve not to turn back and wave at those big kohl lined eyes that seemed as deep as the abyss that threatened to drown him inside.

I want to contain you
Within myself... Said I
The clarity that comes with the realization
And acceptance of love scares you...
And so you drift away—
Away from my essence
Away from life
I smile knowingly
And I rise

CHAPTER 25

Diwali Plans

As Maya watched him walk away, uneasiness settled in her heart. An urge to run after him and stop him fluttered like a butterfly trapped in a tangle of webs in her heart.

'Are you alright, Maya?' Anaya asked seeing the paleness that had appeared on Maya's face.

'Umm... yes', Maya replied in a distracted manner. Anaya realized that perhaps Maya didn't want to talk further about it and launched into a banter about how last night had been fun, and how Rhea had been excited to see all the gifts and toys. Maya nodded her head, smiling at all the right moments, but in her heart she was elsewhere. She wondered if Ansh had been thinking about last night. She grew restless and told Anaya that she was done with her shopping and wanted to get back home as she was not feeling too well. The walk back home was uneventful. She was distracted and preoccupied—thoughts of Vivaan and Ansh played like a fireball in her head. The days that followed crept on with the familiar pattern of going to school, coming back, and getting stuff done for her classes. Monday through Friday, Maya would walk her way to school and back, sometimes deliberately taking the way near to the supermarket, hoping to run into Ansh at some point. But it seemed that he had simply disappeared. She thought of sending him a text message and getting things cleared up, but a tiny voice in her head stopped her from doing so.

Meanwhile, Ansh engrossed himself completely in his work, trying to forget Maya and the need to meet and talk to her again. He was trying so hard to get rid of the memory of the night when he had kissed Maya under the starlit sky. His mother had frequently asked him if everything was all right, or something seemed to bother him. She wanted him to accompany her to Dehradun next week for the Diwali. Mrs. Raheja had been requested by principal of St. Paul's School at Dehradun to join the students at the local orphanage to celebrate Diwali and distribute gifts to the children using the funds they had procured at the fundraiser event. Ansh was in a state of dilemma: he wondered if he would get to see Maya, and yet another part of him told him that he was treading dangerous waters, that he should keep away from Dehradun at all costs. He did not want to complicate things for himself, and perhaps Maya as well. What he felt about Maya was not love—of that he was sure—but he felt a strange need for companionship, of friendship and warmth that he felt whenever he was around Maya.

The school was supposed to close today for the Diwali vacations. There was a strange restlessness that hung in the air—an excitement of the holidays that were impending. Almost a week had passed since she had seen Ansh. Maya realized that if Vivaan had been alive, it was going to be their first Diwali together. Anaya and the other colleagues at school were planning to go to the orphanage and spend some time there while Ansh's mother was there for distributing gifts to the small children that afternoon. Maya wanted to go there as well, but a part of her was scared as hell at the thought that she might meet Ansh there, and so she decided to stay at home. Maya remembered how when she was young, how she used to get all excited about Diwali— as soon as the week started, people started putting on the decorative lights outside their houses. Maya used to feel that she had reached a fairyland where each house welcomed happiness with the vibrant trails of light around them. How busy her mother used to be with the preparations of the small puja that they held each year at their house prior to lighting of the firecrackers. Over the years as Maya grew up, she gave up the idea of bursting firecrackers and found solace in lighting up the earthen lamps—diyas—outside her house to mark the traditional way of celebrating Diwali, driving away the darkness.

Maya had bought earthen lamps and painted them herself. She always found happiness in painting the diyas herself. Maya always made it a point to call her mother on the days of the festivals. It gave her a sense of belonging, peace and happiness. But this year, she seemed lost; she had no one to call. She wondered if this was how Vivaan felt— alone. But he had Ansh beside him, always. And suddenly, she wanted to see him and talk to him. Her dad had called her earlier that day, but the truth was that Maya was still unsure that she could handle the grief that dwelled deep in her heart. She didn't want to break down in front of her 'family.'

The next evening, Maya lightened up the diyas and set them all around the house as the darkness settled in. Anaya had called her sometime back, wishing her Diwali and asking her to come over. But Maya had simply refused, saying that she wanted to stay at home. She had spent the entire morning making sweets and food for the festival. She had been thinking of going to the orphanage tonight with the homemade food and some sweets. She got everything ready and decided to stop by at Anaya's on her way back.

Unaware of her plans, the biggest shock of her life— Ansh stood outside her door, pacing up and down, thinking whether he should ring the bell or simply walk away.

The silence of the night
Smells of loneliness,
Yet the serenity it brings is peaceful...
Your presence is similar to this silence—
Omnipresent, yet
Elusive.
What is it about you that is magic?
The shades of the dark sky—
Or perhaps the beat of the dead city life
What exactly about you is so alluring?
Pulling me into an abyss
Even as I know your presence might be just an
Illusion

CHAPTER 26

Night Lanterns

Maya almost had a heart attack as she opened the door to leave, and almost dropped all the stuff on the ground when Ansh reached out and steadied her.

'Happy Diwali, Maya', Ansh said.

'Happy Diwali', replied Maya.

A deep relief rose in her heart and spreads like warmth through her as soon as she saw Ansh.

'Were you going somewhere?' asked Ansh.

'Oh, yes. I was just going to the orphanage to hand over these sweets that I made and was thinking of stopping by at Anaya's on my way back. Why don't you come along?' she asked.

Ansh agreed and offered to give her a ride. They drove with silence between them, acting as a veil. Each of them lost in their own thoughts. Maya went inside to hand over the sweets to the caretaker of the orphanage. As she walked out, she saw Ansh standing near his car, looking at her. She knew that they needed to talk—talk about Vivaan, about that night and about what was bothering her.

'We need to talk, Ansh', Maya said quietly as she reached him.

'Do you want to go for a walk nearby? This place is quite nice. I came here yesterday for some work with my mother and looked around', Ansh added.

Maya nodded and they fell in step with each other as they walked towards the courtyard where a few children were playing.

'Maya, I am sorry for the other night. I didn't mean to offend you… It… just happened. I was not sure why though. But it did, and it's not your fault, nor mine. I think we both were kind of stressed…' he trailed.

'I know. It's ok. You need not be sorry for what happened. It was a moment that was meant to happen and it did. I don't think that we should keep running away from each other just because we shared something so intense at that moment', replied Maya.

Ansh wanted nothing more than holding her close to his heart and staying there. But he knew that to develop that kind of bond or friendship, they needed time, trust and comfort, which had not developed between them yet.

'So, tell me. How is your life going on? Anaya told me that the school has closed for the Diwali vacations. What are your plans for these holidays?', asked Ansh.

'Ah, I have no special plans, you see. Usually, the school keeps me busy, but since the school is closed now, I actually don't have much to do. Maybe I will read a few books or do stuff I have been planning to do in a while', replied Maya.

'What kind of stuff were you planning to do?' asked Ansh.

'Well, it might sound funny to you but I had been planning to write a book for quite some time now. But I don't know what I should write about yet', continued Maya.

Ansh gave a distracted smile, nodding his head. Maya felt drawn to his smile like a moth is attracted towards the faint glow of the yellow haze.

'What's funny?' she asked.

'I am laughing at my foolishness. I should have known you write. After all, why would Vivaan fall for you, if not words?', Ansh said.

Maya smiled. 'We had planned that someday we would write a book together. But I think, sometimes, things are beyond our control.'

'Write about Vivaan and you—how you met, how everything fell in place, and so on…' offered Ansh.

'I didn't have enough time with him, Ansh. Sometimes, I think I didn't even know him completely. Perhaps, I could write about your and Vivaan's friendship, your childhood and youth. What do you think?' asked Maya.

'Your wish. I can tell you our stories. And if you want to pen them down, I would be more than happy to help,' Ansh smiled.

'I have some of Vivaan's stuff… His diaries, from the days when you both were young. I went through them. Both of you had quite some fun it seems…' Maya said.

'Are you referring to the time in college when we both almost got expelled for smoking right outside our class?' winked Ansh.

Maya rolled her eyes and said, 'And what about the time you both went to that crazy party and got drunk and found yourself on the roadside early morning?'

'Till date, I do not remember what had happened that night, it was so crazy…'

Ansh ended up laughing.

'It's strange that Vivaan never mentioned anything about his struggles in his diaries. None of it mentions the deep unhappiness, the pain that he suffered throughout. Maybe he wanted to remember the happy thoughts alive through his journals...' Maya said.

As their banter continued, both Maya and Ansh felt that a kind of bond was developing between them—a bond of friendship and trust. They felt in their heart a void, remembering the person whom they both loved beyond everything, and felt blessed that they had someone who could completely understand this void Vivaan had left behind in their lives.

When I am around you…
A little light is all I need,
To grow and spread my roots.
A little light
To face this world,
In all its glory…
To stand strong…
To stand alone…
A little light from you is all I want,
And I promise to
Bloom

CHAPTER 27

Doors to Friendship

After talking to Ansh about the book, Maya actually felt an urge to start writing. She wanted to get started soon. She had asked Ansh if he would be in town for the next couple of days. That way she could get started with her story on Ansh and Vivaan's friendship. Ansh had some meetings scheduled for the next few days, but promised to get in touch with her soon. Both of them had started feeling more comfortable talking to each other after their conversation on the Diwali evening. When Ansh called on Tuesday afternoon, Maya was in the middle of reading a book. They decided to meet for coffee at a nearby café.

Ansh felt at peace after speaking to Maya the other night. He had wanted to cancel some of his meetings and stay back and talk to her even the next day. But he knew that if he did that, he might scare her away. Sometimes, it was better to wait for the right time and let things develop by themselves. Ansh was looking forth to the kind of friendship that he and Vivaan once shared.

Ansh had been waiting at the coffee shop for the past fifteen minutes. It was still thirty minutes earlier than the time that they had decided to meet, but Ansh didn't have any prior tasks to be done that evening so he decided to walk over to the shop early. As Maya walked in, wearing a yellow top that she had paired with deep-blue denim, Ansh marveled at her simplicity. Maya came forth and asked, 'Did I keep you waiting for long?'

'No. I came in earlier than we had scheduled to meet', Ansh winked.

'Do you want coffee? I definitely need some at this time of the evening', Maya asked, taking up the menu.

'Yes, I do', Ansh replied.

They continued talking over the cup of coffee. They bonded instantly, talking about stuff Ansh and Vivaan did together—riding bicycles, stealing fruits from the orchards of their school, flying kites, studying for exams together, and staying up late at night. It was amazing how their friendship had blossomed and become deeper with time. Maya thought it was one of the few gifts that she felt that made life worthwhile. Behind these tales, Maya discovered that both Ansh and Vivaan would go to any extent to save the back of the other, if ever such a situation arose. Maya felt excited that she had something to write about now, but she still needed to figure out the story plot and how she would proceed. She wanted that whatever she wrote should be able to reflect the tiniest of thoughts and emotions, and so she needed to be sorted in terms of how she wanted to bring alive the memories on paper—in words.

She spent the rest of the week writing, reflecting on the stories she had heard from Ansh. At times she felt pangs of hopelessness and decided she wouldn't write anymore. At times she felt that she had reached a dead end and that the story would die down. But then, some thought would come to her mind, getting her all excited and then she would write again.

The school was supposed to re-open the next day after the vacations, and she knew that she wouldn't be able to devote much time writing then. She wanted someone to review her writing, read it for her once, and let her know if it was worth anything. Maya remembered that she had never actually written down anything for Vivaan. They didn't have enough time together. She wondered if Ansh would have time to read it.

Ansh's cell phone beeped and Maya's name flashed on the screen. He smiled and opened her text message.

Maya: Was wondering if you are too busy to read what I wrote.

Ansh: Well, I was wondering if you would let me...

Maya: Awesome. Shall I send it to you over e-mail? Now?

Maya's excitement brought a smile on Ansh's face. He was not much of a reader. Vivaan often used to get him books for his birthday, but he seldom bothered to read through them completely. But this was different, he felt Maya had written about him and Vivaan, and he was curious see their friendship reflected through her words.

Ansh: Yes send it to me.

Within moments, his laptop beeped and notified him of a new e-mail. He sprawled out on his bed and began reading.

Maya had been eagerly waiting for Ansh to get back to her and tell her what he thought about her writing. She had been distracted for the entire morning at school. It was indeed lucky that the exams were beginning in two days and there was nothing new to be taught to the students, other than revision and getting them ready for exams. But Maya felt her mind was in a state of turmoil unless she heard back from him. Perhaps it was so trashy that he had given up the idea of reading through it after a few pages. Anaya had asked her twice since morning if everything was okay with her, as she seemed distracted. She had brushed off her questions and said everything was fine and that she was a bit tired, as she hadn't slept well at night—which in fact was the truth. Maya had stayed up the entire night looking at her cell phone hoping to hear back from him.

Three days had already passed and Maya was quite miffed at Ansh. She decided that she would write further and would not let anyone read it. She would write for herself and knew that it would ultimately liberate her thoughts. Ansh could well go to hell by himself.

The storm in your eyes,
Drawing me towards their endless depths
Are subtle,
Making me choke each time I look into them;
For it was not until I looked into them
That I knew what skipping a heartbeat meant.

CHAPTER 28

Realizations

Ansh had never been an avid reader, but he was mesmerized at the way words flowed through Maya's thoughts. He had never thought that he could be so influenced by someone's writings—her words reflected and captured the minor nuances of emotions that simply brought the memories alive. He thought that Maya and Vivaan would have suited each other's quest for words easily. He wondered if they had bonded over words—words that created magic in their lives. He felt how strange it was that the twenty-six letters of the alphabet of the English language had such tremendous ability to influence people, to influence thoughts and the way they felt.

And as he had stayed awake the entire night reading the part of manuscript that Maya had sent to him for reading, he had sensed his feelings change for her. The flow of energy in her writing was so strong that he felt connected to it instantly. Even though her story was set in a village in Ireland in the 18th century, it was the story of two friends Emmet Wilson and Hugh Fiennes, and their memories—beautifully written and narrated from the point of view of a woman they both had fallen in love with, Maggie Parkson.

It was a tale of love and loss. Maggie had been in love with Hugh, but he succumbed to the callings of destiny and he became a victim of crossfire in the local village where he breathed his last. How Maggie survived without him and moved forth in life was reflected beautifully. He felt Maggie's pain was a raw reflection of Maya's own pain. Maggie and Emmet grew closer in the days that followed and became friends. Ansh could see with clarity the striking similarity between their bond and the friendship that was growing between him and Maya. Ansh realized that he was falling in love with Maya—deeply. He was also worried about how she would react if she had an inkling of how he felt for her. He couldn't risk losing her friendship. He decided that he wouldn't tell her how he loved her writing, how he wanted to know how their tale ended, but was afraid at the same time that it would seal the fate of Maya's and Ansh's friendship. He wanted to tell her that her writing style was brilliant, but the he felt she might read too much into his expression.

He felt it was better to let chaos reign, rather than trying to sort out everything. He was still in Dehradun trying to wrap up some work before leaving for Hardwar the next day. He often thought of Maya, but still he held onto his emotions not letting them run wild. After all, he wasn't even sure of what she felt. He was supposed to go and meet Tara next week, and Tara had specifically asked him to get her a letter from Maya.

He decided to take his chances that evening and dropped in to visit her. He was still thinking of walking away when Maya opened the door.

She seemed pleasantly surprised to see him and invited him in.

'So, you still exist?' she jested.

Ansh couldn't help smiling and said, 'I... was a bit caught up with everything. I will be visiting Tara, and she has demanded a letter from you, which brings me here.'

The look that passed on her face was priceless, 'Yes, sure! But you will have to come back for it sometime later. I need time to write. You want tea?' she asked. Maya had piled up her hair in a high ponytail. She never wore any make-up except for the kohl that made her eyes look intriguing.

'Hey?'

Ansh realized that he still hadn't answered.

'Yes, sure. Tea would be great. Had a long day at work,' he replied, walking over to the small garden that extended outside the porch of her house. The garden was small but it was so welcoming. He marveled at all the creativity that Maya kept around her.

'Tea is ready', Maya's voice called in from the kitchen.

They chatted for hours at end, and soon it was almost dinnertime. Maya offered to cook something, but Ansh insisted on going somewhere for dinner. They went to a nearby Chinese place for dinner, and had ice cream to top it all. By the end of it all, Maya was so full that she was ready to collapse. Ansh drove her home and they stood outside her house just looking at the stars talking. And, uninvited, came the memory of the night at Anaya's house and their walk afterwards. Ansh took a step back, ready to leave, when Maya reached out and held his hand...

Her touch was magic...
Awakening spirits that he felt had ceased to exist
Her smile had the calming effect
That could silence a hundred storms that had kept
*   him awake.*
Her silence, however
Unsettled him...
Calm, quiet, intriguing...
Evoking in him a deep sigh
Of having found her...

CHAPTER 29

Finding You

Maya took Ansh by surprise as she stepped closer and hugged him. At first, he simply couldn't respond but gradually, he curved to accommodate her tiny form as they fit into each other. They both felt that something between them had changed. She broke down suddenly and Ansh held her close. He led her inside her house. It was already 2 a.m. and the night had been emotionally tiring for both of them. They kept talking, and soon Ansh found that Maya had dozed off.

He tucked Maya into her bed. It was already quite late and he was so tired that he decided to crash in there. He locked the door and lay on the couch, remembering how gentle Maya had felt against him. One thing he was sure of tonight—that he had fallen in love. He just wanted to tell Tara before he confessed his feelings to Maya. He decided he would tell Maya about his feelings when he came back to get the letter.

He hardly felt he had slept for an hour or so when he felt something brush against his cheek. He knew it was Maya, and he didn't want to scare her off. But as he opened his eyes, he saw the tears in her eyes, and without thinking he pulled her towards himself, his lips searching for hers. He didn't feel that Maya resisted when their lips met. Her soft pliant lips gave way under his. She looked beautiful in the dim light that lit up her room. He knew that he was in love with this woman who looked like an angel at that moment. All his pain, all his emptiness, seemed to have vanished as she laid his head against his chest and fell asleep. This time, a deep and peaceful one.

When she woke up next morning, she found herself snuggled up against Ansh's sleeping form. She felt a strange calmness in her soul. And she realized that she was happy. She had let go of the pain that consumed her after she had lost Vivaan. Today she could remember Vivaan without tears welling up in her eyes. As she tried to get up, Ansh turned and held her in a closer embrace. Though she wanted that moment to last forever, she wasn't sure what would happen when Ansh woke up. They both had been carried away the night before by their emotions. She still had no clue if Ansh loved her.

Maya closed her eyes, and she stifled a cry that seemed to shake her. She felt like crying. It was then she felt Ansh wake up, gently asking her what was wrong.

Not trusting her own voice, she kept her eyes closed and hugged him.

And so Maya and Ansh lay there, wound up around each other, each lost in their own thoughts.

Thoughts that revolved around each other.

And around Vivaan.

Just like the ripples induced on a clam surface
Is shrouded with uncertainty,
Your presence in my memories is uncertain.
Peeking at me in the midst of a busy day.
Making me smile—
At times overwhelming me.
This uncertainty is magical in itself,
Making the journey worthwhile,
Because it is impossible to gauge,
When you will be a part of my soul,
Yet again

CHAPTER 30

Choices

O ver the next few days, Maya completed her story.

Maggie, through her emotional ordeals, had decided to live her life with the memories of her beloved Hugh. She had turned down Emmet's proposal to marry him, but promised to stay friends with him. She wouldn't be able to forget Hugh, she had told Emmet, and that it would be unfair on her part to say yes to Emmet when in her heart she still completely loved Hugh.

After that night, Maya felt that Ansh was deliberately choosing to avoid her. He had still not told her if he had gotten through reading her story. But she still wanted to send it to him and know if he liked it. She decided to send him a text message.

Maya: Hi there?
Ansh: Hey, Maya? I got a bit caught up with work at my end. I didn't get a chance to go through your story yet. I am really sorry.

Maya: It's okay. Do you want to meet sometime? I finished writing the story. You could read it if you still want to.

Curiosity to know what path Maggie chose got the better of him, and he agreed to meet her that night. Maya asked him to come over to her house and have dinner with her. He was still fighting with his own emotions. He wasn't sure what would Maya think if he told her that he loved her, about what he felt for her. How his emotions for her had changed from admiration to pure love. He decided he would tell her what he felt for her that night.

Maya thought of making *palak paneer* for dinner that night. She was still cooking when the doorbell rang, and Maya realized that Ansh had already arrived. She rushed to open the door. Relief spread over her at finally seeing him after such a long time.

'Hey, come in, Ansh', Maya said.

'Did I ever tell you how peaceful this place is? It has this feeling of warmth in it, which seems to call out to people', Ansh said, stepping inside.

Maya smiled and said, 'Thank you. Make yourself comfortable, I am still cooking. I will be done in ten minutes. Do you want anything to drink? Tea or Coffee?'

'No. I just came from office. Had a long day', Ansh said, settling down on the couch that seemed inviting.

Maya went inside the kitchen getting the food ready for dinner. Ansh fumbled around with some books kept on the coffee table, and he saw the manuscript of her book printed out and halfway folded with red marks and crosses on it. Maya must have been proofreading and editing, he thought. He flipped through it and reached the part where she had left, before she had sent it to him to read.

Reading through, Ansh felt a strange rejection in his heart. Maya had made clear the life she would choose for herself through Maggie's tale. He felt his mind would explode and he couldn't stand it anymore. Maya was calling out something to him from the kitchen. He felt that he needed to get a grip on himself and left Maya's house. And without saying a word, he left.

Maya had called out to Ansh twice from the kitchen, but there was no response. She wondered if he was so tired that he had fallen asleep. She went to check on him and found the couch empty. There was no trace of Ansh anywhere. The door was ajar, and she went to check if he was taking a walk outside. But even his car was gone.

Maya tried calling him, but he wouldn't respond. She was confused and bewildered at his behaviour. Why did he leave without saying anything, she thought. As she went inside, she saw the pages of her manuscript, trying desperately to escape from under the weight of the wooden pen stand.

And it was at that moment that she knew.

For
Life found you
To breathe,
To rise—
Not to be bound in a cage.
As you evolve
Live to shine, not for others—
But for eyes that are your own...
For life created you...
As stardust—
To burn bright...

CHAPTER 31

Loving You

Standing outside her house looking up at the stars, Maya thought how amazing it is to love someone so completely and in all entireties that one is not afraid to be left behind. Sometimes, how the longest connections yield very little growth and how at times the briefest of encounters change everything around us. She had learnt in these few years that one couldn't measure love in time. The heart doesn't wear a clock that keeps ticking. She believed that love could bring about transformation. True love was all about resonance. She thought how different everything would be today if Vivaan was still around. Would it change anything? Would her life have taken on a different course? Vivaan had been like an unsolved mystery for her, but being a part of his life had taught her things that no one ever had.

She was getting cold outside and decided to go inside. The smell of freshly brewed coffee wafted in through the air as soon as she stepped inside. Maya smiled as she spotted her pouring out coffee in the two large coffee mugs she had bought just a day back.

'Coffee is here', Tara's voice boomed out to her.

'Coming', Maya said.

As she settled on her favorite spot on the couch, Maya remembered how, after Ansh had left suddenly without saying anything, the realization had dawned on her that she had started falling in love with him and had decided to talk to him the next day. But to her dismay, Ansh had left Dehradun and disappeared. She had gone looking for him at his house in Dehradun, but his mother told her that he had left India for some business trip for a few months.

Ansh's denial of the fact that they both might be in love with each other, together with his decision to walk away from her, had initially made her mad. She had left everything on destiny and thought that if things were meant to be, then they would meet somewhere. She had finally met him a year later at a publishing house, when she was trying to get her book published. Maya was surprised to find him when she had walked in to talk to the CEO of the publishing house. Ansh's father had owned a couple of different businesses, of which this was one. Ansh was actually planning to sell this publishing house and he had come to town to finalize the details about the sale.

'So, you finally finished writing it?' Ansh asked her.

'Yes. I had so much time after you left without dinner that night that I finally completed it', she retorted.

'Well, I had some work and had to leave...' he replied, his voice unsteady.

Maya could see the torment in his eyes. They had not been in contact after that night. Ansh had decided not to be in contact with her.

'Read this, she said thrusting the manuscript in his hand. And read it completely before jumping to conclusions', with that, Maya had walked away.

When he had knocked at her door early next morning, his eyes told her that Ansh had been awake, reading the book. Maya let him in and stayed silent, wanting him to speak.

'You changed the ending of the story', Ansh said.

'You lied that you didn't read it when I had sent it to you', Maya replied.

'I was stupid... I thought that whatever I felt for you had no basis. I thought that denying my feelings would make things easier for you and me...' Ansh trailed as he stepped forth towards Maya and she melted in his arms. He pulled away from her, leaving Maya confused.

'Maya, you don't know anything about me, except the fact that Vivaan was my best friend. You have known me from whatever I have told you about Vivaan me', said Ansh.

'How does it matter, Ansh? Does our connection—our bond—mean nothing? It's not every day that we meet people with whom we connect so well. So deeply.' Maya said.

But Ansh had been non-pliable. He had this unbending thought that his presence in Maya's life would not do any good to her. And even though he confessed to love her, he told her clearly and plainly that he did not want to stay with her.

Tara had tried hard to reason out with him as well, but Ansh could be stubborn as hell. Maya was glad that at least Tara understood her. Maya had tried to get in touch with her dad, tried hard that she could bridge the gap that had developed between them, but she had realized with time that some things are not meant to be. Sometimes, it's the incompleteness of life that makes it what it is.

She still thanked Vivaan for coming into her life and making her realize how beautiful love was. Even though there were parts of him she had not completely understood, she still felt that knowing him had been one of the best gifts she could ever have. Even though Vivaan was gone, he would always be a part of her life—he would always watch over her. As life moved on, she realized how beautiful life itself was. She had stopped evaluating herself in terms of people whom she loved. But that didn't stop her from loving Ansh. She was thankful that she had learnt to love completely without having any inhibitions.

She still believed in the strength of love.

I am willing to love you,
Even if there are parts of you that can't be
reached...
I am willing to reach out,
And stay.
A little bit of faith is all you need,
A little bit of assurance of the fact
That all would be fine.
Let me love you—
Just once.
Amidst the ticking hands of a clock,
Let us be time and memory.
Just for once—
Let 'me and you' be 'us.'
Let us love—
Let us create memories that
Will guide us
Through.

Acknowledgements

For turning a dream into reality, it requires the endeavors and support of people whose faith can drive us forth. I would like to thank all the people who have shown their faith in me at some point. I wish to thank Partridge India for their services. My di has been instrumental in encouraging me to develop this story and being a part of this story as much as me.

This story is very close to my heart; some people and some instances affect us so deeply that they leave a profound impact on us. However, much time passes, however more we learn to move on, we still remember the nuances of emotions that had influenced us in the first place. I wish to thank all the people who have been a part of my life and affected me, influenced me and encouraged me to write.

Special thanks to 'Ansh' for encouraging me, for considering it a worthy attempt and my crazy friends Garima and Chandni for bearing my emotional turbulences while the Story writing process. Special thanks to Hamim da for the cover picture, and Elio and Abhi for the helping me bring to life the book cover concept that I had in my mind.

Thank you and Remember where it all started from.

Sriparna Saha
17th November 2016

Printed in the United States
By Bookmasters